Where The Wild Horses Roam

By
Duane Boehm

Where The Wild Horses Roam

Copyright 2017 Duane Boehm

All rights reserved.

For more information or permission contact:
boehmduane@gmail.com

This book is a work of fiction. References to real people, events, establishments, organizations, or locales are intended only to provide a sense of authenticity and are used fictitiously. All other characters, and all incidents and dialogue are drawn from the author's imagination and not to be construed as real.

ISBN: 1-546-77581-1

Other Books by Duane Boehm

In Just One Moment
Last Stand: A Gideon Johann Western Book 1
Last Chance: A Gideon Johann Western Book 2
Last Hope: A Gideon Johann Western Book 3
Last Ride: A Gideon Johann Western Book 4
Last Breath: A Gideon Johann Western Book 5
Last Journey: A Gideon Johann Western Book 6
Last Atonement: A Gideon Johann Western Book 7
Wanted: A Collection of Western Stories (7 authors)
Wanted II: A Collection of Western Stories (7 authors)

Dedicated to all my nieces and nephews - Rachel, Darren, Kari, Scott, Lakin, Jessica, and Kayla

Chapter 1

You can break a wild horse, but it doesn't mean that you can trust it. At least that's what Caleb Berg's daddy always said. He uttered those words whenever they were working with an ornery horse on their farm outside of Chalksville in west Tennessee. His point being that some animals had a mean streak that you could never tame. They never kept those horses. That's the first thing that came to mind as Caleb watched his sister, Britt, and her two children walking towards the well-used corral where he and his father were working the yearlings. Britt's husband, Charles, had given her another bad beating. One eye was already swelling shut, her nose and lips were dripping blood down onto her dress, and from the way she cradled her right arm, it looked to be broken. Caleb could feel the blood pumping in his temples and a rage building that he had lost control of on more than one occasion.

Britt had never really tamed Charles Roberts, but she had managed to corral him into marrying her against the wishes of the rest of her family. Charles was the same age as Caleb and had been a lout ever since grade school. The wealth of the Roberts family had always kept Charles out of jail and enabled his penchant for drinking and fighting to only grow worse. After the first time that Charles thrashed Britt, Caleb beat his brother-in-law so badly that the whipping put Charles in bed for a week. Caleb spent a month in jail for his deed. Charles stayed on his best behavior for a year after that, but the drinking had eventually started back and only gotten worse.

Britt began crying as her father and brother rushed to her side. "Charles is passed out in a chair on the veranda. He's so drunk that he can barely walk. I think he broke my arm," she said as she held her injured limb against her stomach.

Her daddy put his arm around his daughter and led her towards the house. "Let's get you inside and then we'll take you into town to see the doctor," he said. The two children followed their mother like ducklings in a row.

Caleb's daddy, Nils, made his living as a farmer and lauded horse breeder while his mother, Olivia, worked as a schoolteacher. They were both slow to anger or take actions when wronged. The couple was well respected in the community and known for their hospitality. On occasion, Caleb thought his parents should take more of a stand against some of the shenanigans that went on in Chalksville.

Caleb stomped towards his horse. Anger had taken control of him to the point that revenge was the only thing on his mind. His father called out twice before Caleb heard him and stopped.

"Where are you going?" his daddy asked.

"You know darn well where I'm going. I'll beat him senseless every time he lays a hand on Britt," Caleb said.

"It won't do any good. We need to get her and the children away from Charles," his father said.

"That we do, but he needs to learn his lesson anyways," Caleb said as he grabbed the saddle horn and swung his leg into the saddle.

Caleb Berg stood well over six feet tall with well-muscled arms and shoulders from years of working a plow and training horses. He had turned thirty-three the previous month. During the war, he had fought for Lieutenant Colonel Nathan B. Forrest's Confederate Third Regiment. Under normal circumstances, Caleb was considered an easygoing individual, but he possessed a temper that none of the others in his family had inherited.

His parents always claimed that his disposition came down from his maternal grandfather.

He loped his horse the two miles to the Roberts' home with his mind fixated on the thrashing he would bestow on his brother-in-law. As he rode up the driveway, Charles and Britt's antebellum houses came into view. The couple had one of the nicest houses in the area. The home's clapboard was painted white and it had a wraparound porch with four massive columns and green shutters on every window.

The sound of the pounding hoof beats roused Charles from his slumber. Before Caleb had even begun to pull his horse to a stop, he could see the panic on his brother-in-law's face. Charles wore a sidearm. He wobbled to his feet and drew his revolver.

"Charles, put that gun away before somebody gets killed," Caleb yelled just before the first bullet exploded in his direction.

Caleb hadn't carried a revolver since the war. He pulled his Winchester 73 from the scabbard as a second round whizzed by him. This shot came close enough that he could hear the bullet cut the air. Caleb had treated himself to the new rifle on his past birthday and had been practicing with the gun. His years of fighting in the war had taught him not to panic, but to stay calm and focused in the heat of battle. While Charles desperately fired his third and fourth shot, Caleb took careful aim and fired. His brother-in-law launched backwards and landed in his chair as if he had decided to take a rest. His respite would be forever.

Jumping down from his horse, Caleb walked carefully to the body. He put his fingers against Charles' jugular vein to check for a pulse. His brother-in-law had already passed from a direct hit to the heart. Caleb tried to concentrate on his breathing, taking a couple of deep breaths and trying to release the tension he felt rising up into his chest. Looking around the yard, he decided that no one else was near the house. He dragged the body into the yard to keep blood from dripping down onto the freshly painted veranda floor.

Killing Charles Roberts had been the last thing on Caleb's mind, but his brother-in-law lay as dead as a doornail. Memories of his first kill in the war flashed through Caleb's mind and the same nausea gripped his stomach. After the surrender at the war's end, taking another man's life was about the last thing that he ever thought he would do again. He wanted to jump on his horse to ride back home as if the last few minutes had never happened and make the killing go away.

A decision had to be made, and he knew that whatever he decided, his choice would determine the course to the rest of his life. He could go to town and get the sheriff. That's what he would do if the Roberts' family didn't own and control most everything in Chalksville. After the incident when he had beaten Charles, it had taken all of the sheriff's persuasion to keep the Charles' family from dragging Caleb out of jail and doing God knows what to him. Self-defense would not carry any weight with the Roberts. He held out little hope that the sheriff would stop them this time, and even if they did, he knew that he would never get a fair trial. Judge Claiborne's family and the Roberts family went way back. He'd be sentenced to hang if found guilty and he had no doubt that D.A. Connors would find a jury sympathetic to the Roberts. If he chose to live, he truly had only one option.

After sticking Charles' gun back in its holster, he grabbed Charles' legs at the boots and locked them against his sides as he dragged the body, plow horse style, to the barn and into an empty stall. Using loose hay, he covered the body and the stall floor until satisfied that no hump could be spotted.

Caleb then rode to his own home. The small, framed house had four rooms. Neglected for the past couple of years, the structure begged for a new coat of paint. He walked into his home and looked around the rooms. He knew that he would never again see the place. So many years and memories were lived out inside the walls – some of the best and worst times of his life. Walking to the chifforobe, he grabbed two changes of clothes along with his winter coat and slicker. He stuffed the clothes and all of his cartridges into his saddlebags before rolling the coat into the slicker. As he started to leave, the picture sitting on the mantel of his deceased wife caught his eye. Caleb pulled the picture down and gazed longingly at the photograph for a moment before shoving it into his saddlebag.

Riding back to his parents' house, Caleb went inside the parlor and waited for the family to return from the doctor's office. Mementos from a lifetime of marriage and family filled the room. Melancholy settled over him as he glanced at the pictures on the mantel. From the window, he watched the wagon arrive with his whole family aboard it. Britt's arm was bandaged in a splint, and she stood stiffly when her daddy helped her down from the seat. Caleb could see that her left eye had swelled completely shut and her lips were pursed in pain. Instead of anger, sadness enveloped him - sadness for Britt, her children, his parents, and for himself. Nothing would ever be the same after this day.

"What happened?" Nils asked his son after the family came inside the home.

Caleb made a small nod towards the children.

Britt shepherded her children out the door. "Go play until dinnertime," she said.

Taking a breath, Caleb scanned the faces in the room before exhaling. "Charles shot at me four times. I had to kill him," he said.

"Oh, my God," Britt cried out.

His mother let out a wail.

"Britt, I didn't have a choice. I never went there to kill Charles," Caleb said.

"You should have left well enough alone," Britt yelled as she dropped into a chair and let out a yelp of pain.

"Yeah, so that he could have killed you one of these days," Caleb responded.

"The children don't have a father now," Britt screamed.

"They never had one anyways and you know it. Let's not make a saint out of Charles just because he's dead," Caleb said.

"That's the last thing I intended to do, but he did provide for us," Britt said.

"Britt, I never meant to kill him. He woke up on the porch and started shooting. You believe me don't you?" Caleb asked.

"Of course, but whether he was good for nothing or not, I'm still a widow," Britt said.

"Enough," Nils ordered. "You need to go to town and tell the sheriff what happened."

"Daddy, Charles' brothers and father tried to drag me out of jail the last time. They'll kill me this time one way or the other. You know with the way that they control things around here that a grand jury will bring it to trial and I'll be found guilty. Judge Claiborne will hang me. They always get their way. I'm a dead man if I don't run," Caleb said.

"We're a good Christian family. You can't run away like some outlaw. The killing was self-defense," Nils said.

Olivia stepped forward. "Caleb is right. He will never get a fair trial. I will not have my son hanged for the likes of Charles Roberts. We're a family and we take care of our own. Charles has been a blight on us since the day he married Britt," she said.

Silence fell over the room. Britt looked as if she were trying to comprehend how a run of the mill day had turned into such a disaster. Nils and Olivia seemed at a loss for words.

"Momma is right. I didn't want Charles dead, but we all know that he didn't amount to anything. I stopped loving him a long time ago. He beat me and ignored the children. Something really bad would've happened one of these days – maybe even to one of the kids. I'll not be a party to Caleb hanging," Britt said.

"I hid the body in a barn stall under some hay. Give me a day and then go to town to tell the sheriff that Charles and I are missing. That should give me enough distance to evade the posse," Caleb said.

"Where will you go?" Olivia asked her son.

"I guess out west. Nobody will know me out there and I've always wanted to see the mountains," Caleb said.

"We'll never see you again," his mother said and hugged her son.

"I'm going to tell Tyler and Sissy goodbye," Caleb said.

"No, you can't. They're too young to understand. They might say something to incriminate us. We can't take the chance," Nils said.

With a stroll to the window, Caleb watched the two children while they played. He adored both of them. A pang of loss for all he was leaving behind washed over him. "I'm going to miss them," he said, his voice breaking.

Britt stood gingerly and walked over to her brother, grabbing his hand. "Caleb, you need to go somewhere and start over your life. You used to be so happy before Robin died. You've never gotten over losing her and the baby. Sadness hangs on you like ill-fitting clothes. You need to find the old you. I'll pray for your safety and a new life," she said.

Nils turned to his wife. "Momma, go get your scissors and help Caleb cut off that beard. I'll warm some water for shaving," he said before scurrying away.

Caleb's beard hung down to his chest. A razor hadn't touched his face since leaving for the war. He took a seat and his mother walked towards him with her scissors gnashing. She cut his beard as close to the skin as she dared. Hair littered the floor when she finished. With the water hot, Caleb lathered his face and picked up his father's razor. The act of shaving felt as foreign as if he were attempting to do it left handed as he glided the razor across his face.

After finishing, he wiped his face with a towel and gazed at himself in the mirror. He looked so much younger with the beard gone and his brown piercing eyes were the focus of his face now. Grinning at his new look in spite of the situation, he could barely recognize himself and decided that he would let his blond hair, already getting long from an overdue haircut, grow out.

"You look like my boy that left for the war," Olivia said, remembering the time before her son joined the Confederate army. The family was the only one of Swedish descent anywhere in the area and Caleb had towered over most of the boys his age that were of Irish, Scottish, and English ancestry. Her good-looking son and had once been a carefree boy always popular with the girls.

Nils walked to the buffet and removed a leather pouch. "There's ten twenty-dollar gold pieces in here. Take it. You'll need money," he said.

"Daddy, I can't take your money," Caleb said.

"I don't want to be worrying about you starving. I insist," his father said as he shoved the pouch into his son's hand.

"Thank you," Caleb said as he reluctantly accepted the money.

"I also want you to take Leif. There's not a horse within a hundred miles of here that can keep up with him. As long as you keep moving, they'll never catch you," Nils said.

Caleb's father had found success crossing Arabian and Quarter horses. He produced stock that retained much of the speed of the Quarter horse with the endurance of the Arabian. His horses were highly desired. People were willing to place their name on a waiting list to purchase one of the animals. Leif was his prized stallion. The dark bay horse stood fifteen and a half hands tall with a temperament as gentle as any gelding.

"He's your favorite and your stallion. I couldn't take him," Caleb said.

"Erik is going to be as good as his daddy. I'll just use him. I can always breed more horses. Momma and I are too old to make another son. It is settled. You need to get moving," his father said.

Britt walked up and hugged her brother. "I love you and I know that you never planned to kill Charles. God's speed," she said.

Hugging his mother, Caleb said, "I'll get word to you when I get settled somewhere. Don't worry about me. I'll be fine. I love you and I'm sorry for all the shame I caused the family."

"You were only looking out for your sister. Be careful and make us proud. I love you," Olivia said as she handed him a sack of biscuits and salt pork. "You'll get hungry and won't have time to hunt."

Caleb shook his father's hand. "Daddy, you take care. You always wanted to see the west. Maybe someday you can come visit me. I love you," he said.

His father embraced him. "Stay good and keep us proud. You're a good son," he said.

"I'll call the children in while you go out the back," Britt said before walking stiffly to the front room.

Making a quick exit of the house before he started crying, Caleb walked to the barn and bridled Leif. He pulled the saddle off his horse and put it on the stallion. Leif made for a fine riding horse as far as stallions go, but he could be a handful around mares. He climbed onto the horse and headed down the driveway. A long night awaited him.

Chapter 2

After looping around Chalksville, Caleb put Leif into a lope, heading west and a little to the north down a little used dirt road. The horse regularly received exercise and could go for miles before getting winded. They traveled for an hour before Caleb pulled the horse into a walk. A long ride stretched ahead and keeping the animal in top condition would be imperative.

They reached the Obion River south of where its last fork joined the tributary. Caleb rode north along the bank until he came to two sandbars catty-corner on either side. He rode out onto the sandbar and aimed for the one on the other side. The water always ran shallower at these points and he made it across without getting his boots wet.

The Mississippi River lay a few miles farther ahead. Caleb wanted to cross before bedding down for the night. An hour later, he came upon the river and followed it north. His daddy and he had ridden to a little town named Hathaway a few years ago to buy a horse and he remembered that it sat a few miles upriver. As he traveled, dusk settled over the landscape, and he feared that he wouldn't get to cross the river that night.

As Caleb neared the town, he spotted an oil lantern hanging from a crooked pole at the river's edge. He considered himself lucky to have managed to reach the outskirts of Hathaway without encountering a single soul. An old, white-haired, black man sat below the light, hunched over and asleep. He jumped up at the sound of the hoof beats, revealing bib overalls that had been patched so many times that they looked like a quilt and a shirt with holes in the elbows.

"Twenty-five cents to cross the river," the man called out before even seeing Caleb.

The wooden raft appeared just big enough for a team of horses with a buckboard wagon and looked to have seen better days. The river could be seen passing under a hole in the floor and the rails were mostly missing.

"Is that thing safe?" Caleb asked as he climbed down from his horse and walked over to the old man. The light from the lamp illuminated the man's face. His irises were faded with age and the whites of his eyes were lined with broken blood vessels. He had lived a long life and looked ancient.

"Sir, I've been using this here raft for going on ten years and I've never lost no passenger yet. My name is Isaac. Pleased to meet you," the man said.

"Well, Isaac, I hope that I'm not your first man overboard," Caleb said as he fetched coins from his pocket and handed them to Isaac.

Leif didn't appear to be too enthusiastic about the raft either and took some nudging to get him to step aboard the rickety thing.

Isaac grabbed his pole and pushed them off the bank and into the current. "Are you going into Gayoso for some refreshment?" he asked with a smile. "If I get any customers this time of day, that's what it's usually for. Later on, I wait on the other side to bring them back home."

"No, can't say that I'm in need of refreshment. Are there any other rafts or ferries near here?" Caleb asked.

"No, sir, least ways that I's knows of," Isaac said as he guided his raft.

"Were you a slave, Isaac?" Caleb asked out of curiosity.

"Sure enough was. I got the scars on my back to prove it. Master Jensen ran a big plantation and he was a mean one. I don't got much, but it's mine now," Isaac said. He straightened his posture and pulled back his shoulders. "Did you fight to keep me a slave?"

"I did fight, but not to keep you a slave. We sure never had any. I guess it was to defend our way of life. I'm not really sure anymore," Caleb answered.

Isaac nodded his head. "It don't matter nows anyways. I'm a free man," he said.

"On which side of the river do you live?" Caleb asked.

"I lives on the Missouri side. Got me a little cabin over there," Isaac said.

"Are you an honest man, Isaac?" Caleb asked.

"Yes, sir. I don't got much, but I does got my honesty. God has kept me alive all these years and I don't aim to disappoint Him now," Isaac said.

Caleb smiled at the old black man. He liked him. "If you don't mind me asking, how much do you usually make a day?" he asked.

"I doesn't mind. I make a dollar on a good day. Most times less," Isaac answered.

"Do you think a twenty dollar gold piece could keep you and your raft on the Missouri side for a week?" Caleb questioned.

"Is the money come by honest?" Isaac asked.

"Yes, it is. Earned the hard way," Caleb answered.

Isaac smiled, his face lit by the moonlight. "I could have me a little rest and relaxation. Buy the missus a present and catch me some big ole catfish," he said.

"You got a deal. I'll fetch your money when we reach the other side," Caleb said.

They reached the Missouri side of the river without incident. Caleb led Leif off the raft and reached into his saddlebag for the pouch of money. He retrieved a gold coin and handed it to Isaac.

"Much obliged," Isaac said with a big smile.

"Thank you. Glad to make you acquaintance. You take care and don't spend all your money in one place," Caleb said as he mounted his horse.

"No, sir, don't you worry about that. I'll squeeze that eagle until she squawks," Isaac said and laughed.

Caleb rode towards Gayoso and found a road that split to the northwest. He followed it, riding for a couple of hours in the dark. The events of the day were wearing on him and he tired from the emotional toll. His brother-in-law and he had always had an uneasy relationship, especially after the beating Caleb gave him, but Caleb had never envisioned in his wildest imagination that he would kill Charles. The killing weighed heavy on him and he felt as if he could ride no farther. He came to a grassy spot on the side of the road and made a cold camp, eating some of the biscuits and salt pork his mother had given him, and washing the food down with water from his canteen. After unrolling his bedroll, he stretched out on the ground and soon fell into a heavy sleep, dreaming of his deceased wife, Robin.

As Caleb awoke with the first light of dawn, he scarfed down a couple of biscuits before resuming his journey. He continued on a northwest path, riding through several small villages and passing by field after field of cotton and corn planted in the rich, black gumbo soil. Whenever he encountered another person, he'd give them a quick nod and keep riding.

Towards evening, he rode through a little town that he wasn't even sure of its name. A little café on the square caught his eye and he stopped in for his first hot meal in two days. A cute waitress tried to flirt with him, but he only smiled at her and kept his conversation to a minimum. As he ate, his mind drifted to his daddy and the realization that at that very moment, his father probably stood in the jail telling the sheriff that he and Charles were missing. After paying for his meal, he left the town and rode until dark.

The next morning, Caleb rode into Poplar Bluff, Missouri. In front of the gunsmith shop, the shopkeeper swept the dust from the boardwalk and eyed Caleb as he dismounted and approached him.

"What can I do for you?" the shopkeeper asked.

"I'd like to buy a revolver. I'm partial to Colt," Caleb answered.

"Is that a Winchester 73 in your scabbard?" the man asked.

"It is," Caleb said.

"I think I have just the thing for you," the owner said as he led Caleb into his store. "Colt just came out with a new version of the Single Action Army in the 44-40 caliber. Same as your Winchester. They call it the Colt Frontier. You only need one size cartridge that way. I just got a couple in last week."

Caleb picked up each of the guns and pointed them at the twelve on the clock. He liked the balance of the longer barreled one. "How much?" he asked.

"Eighteen dollars and I'll throw in a box of shells," the storekeeper said.

"I'll take it. Do you have a gun belt to fit it?" Caleb asked.

"I sure do. Come over here. I have a rack of them that you can pick from," he said.

Looking through the selections, he tried on a plain brown gun belt. The belt fit well and had a leg-tie, hammer loop, and would carry twenty cartridges. He put the new Colt into the holster and tested the fit. "I haven't worn one of these things since the war. It feels kind of odd now," Caleb said.

"Are you expecting trouble?" the shopkeeper asked.

Caleb eyed the storekeeper for signs of suspicion, but saw none. "No, I'm just traveling and want something I can get to quicker than a rifle if the need arises," he said.

He paid the gunsmith twenty-five dollars for the gun, holster, and two additional boxes of cartridges before riding away on Leif. With the gun strapped to his side, he continued to feel strange and constantly gripped the revolver to reassure himself that the gun still rested in the holster.

The countryside began to change on the other side of the town as he entered the foothills of the Ozark Mountains. After a few more hours of riding, he was deep into the Ozarks and his speed of travel slowed dramatically as the trail climbed mountains, and wound and dipped through hollows. His belly started to growl and he wished that he had stocked up on supplies. He hadn't expected the little villages to disappear so suddenly.

Caleb lumbered up the trail on a steep incline. Halfway to the top, a little old lady jumped out of the brush brandishing a shotgun pointed in his direction.

"You're trespassing. Don't do something foolish or I'll blow you out of the saddle," she said.

He raised his hands slowly and studied the woman. She appeared to be in her seventies and her gray hair looked frizzy and wild, going in every direction. Her legs were covered with trousers and she wore a plain dress over the top of them cinched up with a belt.

"I thought that this was a public trail," Caleb said.

"Well, it cuts through my land," she said.

"Are you in the habit of stopping everyone that comes through here?" Caleb asked.

The old woman smiled for the first time. "No, just the ones that I want to stop. And I wanted you. My name's Alice. Get down from your horse," she said.

Even with the shotgun aimed his way, he didn't really fear the old woman. She didn't strike him as a killer. He figured that she would demand a toll and let him go. Climbing down from Leif, he put his hands back in the air.

"My name's Caleb in case you kill me. Well, Alice, what do you want?" he asked.

"Put your hands down and follow me," Alice demanded.

"I need to keep moving," Caleb protested.

"Nobody knows where you are. You have plenty of time," Alice said.

Caleb paused, watching Alice walk away, and wondered what she meant by her statements. She took off through the brush and he followed, leading the horse down the maze of the side trail.

"Aren't you afraid that I'll shoot you in the back?" he asked.

She chortled. "Do you really think that I would've stopped you if I thought you'd shoot me?" she asked.

"What do you want?" Caleb asked in exasperation.

"You looked hungry and I was lonesome for some conversation," Alice said.

"What? This is about a meal and company? You could have just asked if I were hungry," he protested.

Alice let out a cackle. "What's the fun in that? I like to liven things up now and then. Keeps me young," she said.

They reached a little cabin in the middle of the woods. Smoke bellowed from the chimney and a large coon dog rested on the porch beside a stack of firewood.

"The meat should just about be ready," Alice said.

After tying Leif to a sapling in the yard, Caleb followed Alice into the cabin. The room smelled of cooking meat and looked neat and homey. A small table with two chairs sat by the window.

Alice grabbed a towel and fetched the pot from the fire before plopping it down on the table. Meat, potatoes, and carrots bobbled in the bubbling stew. After retrieving plates, spoons, and two cups of water, Alice proceeded to scoop generous portions onto the plates. "Have yourself a seat," she said.

Sitting down, Caleb asked, "Do you force people to eat with you often?"

"Just when the mood strikes me," she said with a laugh.

Caleb's belly ached with hunger and the food tasted wonderful. He tried to pace himself so as not to appear to be a pig scarfing down his food. "This food hits the spot. What kind of meat is it?" he asked.

"Raccoon. That's why I got a coon dog," Alice said with a smile.

Trying not to grimace, Caleb could feel the corners of his mouth curl up at the mention of the food. "Oh," he said.

"Tasted pretty good until you knew what it was, huh?" Alice said with a smirk.

"It still tastes good as long as I don't think about it too hard," Caleb said and tried to smile. "Why did you pick me?"

"I know a farm boy when I see one. Those muscles come from working a farm. Outlaws and such tend to be scrawny from living their life on the run. You're on the run now from something you got yourself into and you looked like you could use a meal," she said.

Caleb stopped chewing in mid-bite and looked at Alice. "Are you a witch or something?" he asked.

Alice let out a loud cackle and slapped the table. Her laugh made the hair on the back of Caleb's neck stand on end and he looked at her warily.

"I'm something all right. I'm old and have seen a thing or two in my time. I see a farmer on the road that should be home tending to his crop this time of year, wearing a new gun that he probably hasn't even shot yet, and riding a horse finer than any I've seen around here. That tells me that somebody got into trouble and just left home," she said.

Taking a drink of water, Caleb did not answer.

"I knew I was right. I bet you killed somebody in a family dispute. It has to be family to cause you to do something so out of character," Alice said.

"You sure think that you know an awful lot about me," Caleb said to kill the uncomfortable silence.

"I knew it. You can't deny me because you can't lie. A brother-in-law, I bet. It's always the bad brother-in-law," she said.

Caleb's expression failed to conceal the astonishment he felt. Alice sat before him smiling like the star of the piano recital. He had no idea whether she was just incredibly lucky at guessing or possessed some kind of ability to read minds. "That's amazing," he finally said.

"Don't worry. I'd never give you away," she remarked.

"What's your story?" Caleb asked.

"I'm just an old mountain woman that's lived around these here parts all my life. My husband died a few years ago and things get lonesome sometimes. Never had any babies to worry over," she said.

"So you spent your time figuring out people," he said.

Alice chuckled. "I guess you could say that or that I'm just plain nosey. Something like that," she said.

"Thanks for the food. It hit the spot," Caleb said.

"Caleb, would you like some advice?" Alice asked.

"What's that?" he asked, unsure where the conversation would lead.

"That pain that you're carrying around that you've buried so deep that you pretend like it doesn't matter anymore – let it go and get on with your life. Eyes are the windows to the soul and yours are about as easy to see through as fresh washed panes at the general store," she said.

Caleb looked Alice in the eyes and tried to stymie the emotion that wanted to break loose and overwhelm. Forcing a wiseass smile onto his face, he said in a cavalier voice, "And what would I be hiding?"

"See you're doing it now. It has to be love and a broken heart. I just don't know how bad," Alice said.

With the battle lost, his eyes welled with tears and he clenched his lips tightly. He made a quick swipe of his face with his sleeve. "She died giving birth to our daughter. Lost the baby too," he said.

"Don't let your tragedy be your view of your world. I'm sure that she'd want you to move on with your life and be happy. I can tell that you haven't been that for a long time," she said.

Minutes passed with the only sounds being their breathing and eating. They finished the meal and still nobody spoke.

Caleb cleared his throat. "It's hard getting over something like that. It changes you, but I'll not forget your words," he said.

"Good. That's a start. You're still young - let go of the past and I bet you'll find love again. I know that if I were a whole lot younger that I'd lay claim to you. Thank you for your company," Alice said. She walked over to an ancient buffet, opening a drawer and retrieving a braided leather bracelet. "I make these sometimes to pass the time. I want you to wear this to remember me and what I told you. I see better days ahead for you." She tied the bracelet onto his left wrist without asking permission and admired her handiwork when finished.

"Thank you. I think I'm the one that got the most out of our meal together. I best be going. I got a long ways to go," he said as he arose from his chair.

He walked Leif back to the main trail and rode away. The encounter had been so strange that he could almost convince himself that it had been a dream if not for his full belly and the bracelet he now wore. Nudging Leif into a lope once they were on the downside of the mountain, he wondered if fate or coincidence had sent Alice and her shogun his way for guidance.

Chapter 3

Britt and the children remained at her parent's home. On the day after the beating, she had been so sore that she barely strayed from her room and her left eye remained completely swollen shut. On the following day, she forced herself out of bed and joined the family for breakfast. Her arm ached something terrible, but she put on a brave face and tried to act her normal self as her children watched her with worry etched on their little faces. All the turmoil that had transpired in the preceding days still lay heavy on the family and the normally jolly meal proved to be a solemn affair.

As Nils arose from his seat to go outside, he looked at his daughter and said, "After lunch we need to talk."

Britt nodded her head as she watched her father turn for the door looking as if all the weight of the world were upon his shoulders.

Nils returned to the house at noon, and after the meal, sent the children out to play. "I've been thinking things over all morning. I think Britt and I need to take the wagon to her place as if we were taking her back home. We'll then ride to Caleb's place and then return home. That way there will be wagon tracks to back my story, and in case anybody sees us, Britt will be with me. I'll head to town and tell the sheriff what we found. I'm going to tell him that Caleb worked here yesterday until suppertime. As long as nobody recognized Caleb out on the road, our story should hold. With two days' worth of tracks on the roads, they'll never even be able to figure out which way he rode. What do you two think?" he asked.

"What about Caleb's horse?" Olivia asked her husband.

"I turned him out with the other geldings. That sheriff would be lucky to recognize his own horse in a herd. They have no reason to go in the barn to see that Leif is gone," Nils replied.

"Are you able to ride on the wagon?" Olivia asked her daughter.

"I have no choice. I'll be fine," Britt answered.

As he grabbed his hat, Nils said, "I'll go hitch the wagon. We have to remember to stick with our story no matter what the sheriff asks," he said.

Nils had to practically lift his daughter up onto the buckboard wagon. As they traveled down the road, each bump would cause Britt to wince in pain. She covered her mouth with her hand so tightly that her cheeks began to go numb.

"Nothing is ever going to be the same again, is it?" Britt finally asked.

"No, it's not," Nils answered.

"This is all my fault. If I would have listened to you and Momma, none of this would have happened," Britt said.

"You were young and in love. We all make mistakes. You can't get through life without making some," Nils said.

"But this one had big consequences," Britt replied.

"Feeling guilty won't change a darn thing and you do have two wonderful children from Charles. Caleb has himself to blame too. He should have thought things out better before riding to your house. That temper of his got him into trouble this time. Do you have a will?" Nils asked.

"Yes, when Charles was trying to get back in my good graces after the first time he beat me, I made him get a will. Everything is left to me. I made him use Thomas Jacobs as our lawyer too. Mr. Jacobs isn't beholden to the Roberts family and they say he writes a will so thorough that other lawyers won't contest it," Britt answered.

"That's good," Nils said.

At Britt's home, Nils climbed down from the wagon and made the pretense of trying to find Charles. He noticed a few drops of blood on the veranda as he walked to the front door. Afterwards, they rode to Caleb's home and he again walked around the place as if trying to find his son. They then returned home. All the riding had caused Britt so much pain that her eyes were welling with tears as her father lifted her off the wagon.

"Put the children in a bedroom if you see the sheriff coming and make sure they stay there," Nils instructed his daughter.

"Yes, Daddy," Britt said before walking to the house.

Nils saddled his favorite gelding and headed to town. By the time he arrived at the sheriff's office, it was nearing suppertime. He found the sheriff sitting at his desk looking as if he were counting the time until he ate. Nils didn't consider Sheriff Briar a bad fellow, but the lawman had a reputation as not the sharpest tool in the shed or the sturdiest.

"Nils, what brings you to town?" Sheriff Briar asked.

"I'm not sure if you are aware that Charles beat Britt again on Thursday ..." Nils began.

"First I've heard of it. Why didn't somebody come get me?" Sheriff Briar interrupted.

"Because you never did anything about it the last time. The doctor had to set her arm this time. If you would have done something, Caleb never would have gone to jail for handling the situation," Nils said testily.

"What's your point for being here?" the sheriff asked in a gruff voice.

"Britt stayed with us afterwards. I took her home today and Charles was nowhere to be found. There were some drops of blood on the veranda. With what happened the previous time, we went to look for Caleb. He's missing too," Nils said.

Sheriff Briar leaned back into his chair and seemed taken aback by the news. "What about their horses?" he finally asked.

"Charles' horse is in the corral. Caleb's is gone," Nils replied.

As he rubbed his forehead with his fingers, the sheriff asked, "When is the last time you saw Caleb?"

"He left our place after supper last night. I wasn't expecting to see him today. He usually spends Saturday taking care of his own place," Nils answered.

"Did you check with Charles' old man or brothers?" Sheriff Briar inquired.

"No, we're not exactly on good terms after all that's already happened," Nils said.

"Dang, my mouth was watering for some roast beef over at the café. I guess I need to find Deputy Hawks and ride out there. You better come along with us," the sheriff said.

The three men rode to the Roberts home. Dusk started setting in just as they arrived. Nils showed the sheriff the blood and they searched inside the house before walking towards the barn.

"Did Caleb say anything about doing Charles harm?" Deputy Hawks asked.

"I told him to stay out of it this time," Nils replied.

Inside the barn, the sheriff noticed all the hay piled in the one stall. He walked into the enclosure, shuffling his feet as he moved and nearly tripped when his boots hit Charles' body. As he scattered the hay, Charles' colorless face came into view. The sheriff blew out a loud breath and said, "Oh, damn, this is not good."

Deputy Hawks and Nils joined the sheriff. The deputy struck a match and scattered some more hay off the body.

"Looks like a shot right to the heart," the deputy noted.

Sheriff Briar reached down, pulling Charles' revolver from the holster. He opened the cylinder and checked the loads. "Four empty casings," he said.

"Sounds like self defense if Caleb is the one that did this," Nils stated.

"How so?" the sheriff asked.

"Because if Caleb planned on killing him, I believe he would be smart enough to do it without getting shot at four times," Nils said.

"Why would he run then?" Deputy Hawks asked.

"First off, I don't know that Caleb is on the run or that he did this, but if he did, I imagine he feared that the Roberts family would either lynch him or that Judge Claiborne would make sure he was found guilty. Let's not pretend we don't know how things work around here," Nils said.

The sheriff returned the gun to the holster. "I wish we could find Caleb and he had a good alibi, but I think we all know that is unlikely. I even suspect that your theory is correct. Charles must have been shot on the veranda and I didn't see any other bullet holes. Charles didn't fire four times after that shot to the heart. Caleb doesn't strike me as a cold-blooded killer anyways, no matter the situation. But if he's on the run, I'll have to charge him with murder. Let's head to his place," he said.

By the time they reached Caleb's home, darkness had fallen over the land. The sheriff lit an oil lamp and walked around the home before heading to the barn to have a look.

"I think it's safe to say that Caleb is on the run," Sheriff Briar stated.

With resignation is his voice, Nils said, "I fear you are right."

"Nils, you can go on home. There's nothing that can be done tonight. I might have to come talk to Britt tomorrow.

Please give her my condolences tonight. I'll send the undertaker out in the morning to get the body. I don't want to deal with the Roberts clan tonight. They can find out things tomorrow," the sheriff said before mounting his horse.

With a touch of his heels into his horse's ribs, Nils put the animal into a trot and headed home. He arrived to find his wife and daughter sitting at the kitchen table. The stress on their faces and the tension in the air was palpable. They both looked up at him as if they were too afraid to ask what had gone on that day.

"Where are the children?" Nils asked.

"We put them to bed early," his wife answered.

"Okay, good. The sheriff found Charles' body and believes Caleb killed him. I planted the seed that it might be self-defense when Sheriff Briar discovered that Charles had fired his gun four times. The sheriff didn't seem too thrilled with trying to find Caleb. I think deep down he thinks that Charles probably got what he deserved. Sheriff Briar might come out here tomorrow and you'll have to go to town sometime to make arrangements for Charles' burial. I think the Roberts will make more effort to find Caleb than the sheriff," Nils said.

"They are nasty people," Britt said.

"Caleb should be long gone. That boy survived that awful war and he knows how to take care of himself," Nils said before looking at his wife. "Momma, I'm about starved."

Chapter 4

Three days after his encounter with Alice, Caleb would think about her every time he looked down at his wrist and saw the leather bracelet that she had given him. He still wasn't sure what to make of her or whether their meeting had been anything more than random chance, but he found that he took some comfort in her advice. Crossing paths with Alice would certainly go down as one of the most unusual experiences in his life so far.

When he wasn't thinking about Alice, he thought about his family. He had usually seen his parents every day and his sister and her kids at least a couple times a week. All of the silence while riding added to his realization that he missed them terribly and might never see them again.

He had ridden through the most rugged parts of the Ozarks and was making better time now. So far, he hadn't seen any signs of being trailed by a posse and he relaxed more each day. At a little village, he had stopped to buy supplies. And he had managed to shoot a couple of rabbits so that he had a decent meal each night.

As he topped a ridge, Caleb could see the trail far ahead descend into a valley. At the bottom of the basin, something pink moved along the road. With his curiosity piqued, Caleb rode on down the hill. When he got closer, he decided that the object looked to be a man wearing only faded red long underwear and a derby hat.

The man stopped and turned towards Caleb as the horse and rider overtook him.

"Are you a robber?" the man asked.

Pulling Leif to a stop, Caleb crossed his wrist over the saddle horn and smiled. "Well, if I were, I'd say that the pickings were a little slim. I'm not in the habit of wearing other people's underwear and I don't think that you're my size anyways. And I don't look good in derbies," Caleb said.

"You wouldn't find this so amusing if the tables were turned. Three men robbed me yesterday. They took everything I had and they weren't my size either, but they seemed to take considerable pleasure in robbing me of my clothes all the same. I lost a good horse and rifle too. It made for a long night. By the way, my name is Joey Clemson," the man said.

Joey looked to be in his early fifties. He stood medium height and thin. His face and hands were brown and weathered from exposure to the sun and he looked to have worked most of his life in the outdoors.

"How can I help?" Caleb asked.

"Springfield is up the road a piece. If I could ride with you and you spot me the money to send a telegram, my boss would advance me money to get a horse and such. I'd pay you double your cost," Joey said.

"No, I'm not in the habit of profiting from other's misfortune. I'll give you the money so that I can be on my way, but I'm not sure that I want to be seen on a horse with a man in his underwear. It could hurt a man's reputation with the ladies," Caleb said.

"I'll hop off and walk when we get to the edge of town," Joey pleaded.

"I was only joshing you. I'm Caleb. I'm not sure how Leif will feel about two riders. He's only had little children ride double," Caleb said.

"I only weigh a hundred and forty. That big brute shouldn't even notice the difference. That's a fine looking horse that you have there," Joey said.

Caleb kicked his foot out of the stirrup and held out his arm. Joey put his foot in and Caleb helped pull him up onto the saddle behind the cantle. Leif nickered and started walking sideways.

Tugging on the reins, Caleb said, "Easy, Leif. You're okay." He nudged the horses in the ribs and they were on their way.

"So where are you headed?" Joey asked after a while.

"Don't really know. I guess I'll figure it out when I get there," Caleb answered.

"I'm from Shawneetown, Illinois. I first came out west on this trail in 1846. I've lived around Fort Laramie in the Wyoming Territory most of those years except for my years in the war. I came back to visit my mom. I hadn't been home in years and she's getting old," Joey said.

"Did you fight for the Union?" Caleb asked.

"I did. How about you?" Joey asked.

"I fought for the Confederacy. We might have shot at each other sometime," Caleb said.

"If we did, I guess it's a good thing for me that we missed," Joey said.

"Yup," Caleb answered.

Both of the men were content to drop the subject of the war without a debate or discussion of the battles that they had fought.

"I work on a horse ranch in the foothills outside of Fort Laramie. We sell horses to the army and cattle ranchers. The ranch has a reputation for producing horses that aren't skittish in battle and for some of the finest cutting horses around the area. I should already be back there. Weather delayed me a couple of weeks. I'll never hear the end of it if I'm not back for the spring roundup. My boss, she's always looking for somebody that knows horses. Being good with a gun sure never hurts either. There are not many people with that combination of skills that wants to be a ranch hand," Joey said.

"She?" Caleb questioned.

"Yeah, Caroline took over the ranch when the Indians got her pa. She married some fool that thought he'd have any easy life with her pa gone. He found out that a ranch is a lot of work, at least with her running things, and he ran off with some jezebel. It kind of soured Caroline on men. She's honest and pays a fair wage, but back in the day, she used to be fun to be around. Not so much anymore," Joey said.

"Horseflesh is one thing that I do know. That and growing corn and cotton. I'm a pretty fair shot with a rifle and I just bought this revolver. I've barely shot one since the war, but I used to have a knack for hitting what I aimed at. I'm still trying to get the feel back for shooting one," Caleb said.

"So are you interested in a job?" Joey asked.

"I don't know. I'm not sure that your boss sounds like somebody I'd like to work for. Why would it matter if I'm good with a gun?" Caleb asked.

"We haven't had trouble in a long time, but it's always handy to have somebody that can hit what they aim at if the need arises. The Indians are still known to get riled up now and then. You and I could ride out to the ranch together and you could decide then. Two people traveling together are a lot safer than one. I know the way and where to find good water. I've seen whole wagon trains sick from drinking bad water," Joey said.

"I'll think about it. The other ranch hands might talk if they knew we shared a horse with you in your underwear," Caleb teased.

"I assure you that nobody at the ranch will ever know that part of the story," Joey said.

Caleb called it a day earlier than usual for fear of taxing Leif with the extra weight. As he unsaddled the horse, the idea dawned on Caleb to let Joey wear his slicker. The coat looked huge on the cowboy, but it beat seeing him in his underwear. Grabbing his rifle, Caleb took off into the brush to hunt while Joey started a fire. A half-hour later, the roar of the Winchester signaled the end of a rabbit's life.

As they sat around the fire eating the rabbit and hardtack, Caleb asked, "How much farther until Springfield?'

"I'd say about ten miles give or take a couple," Joey answered.

"How long do you think that it'll take to get your money wired back?" Caleb inquired.

"Tomorrow is Wednesday and Caroline usually goes to town then. If we're lucky, maybe only a couple of hours," Joey replied.

"I have enough money that we can get you some clothes and we can go to the livery stable and pick out a horse before the money comes in," Caleb said.

"Much obliged. I'd really be in a pickle if you hadn't come along and helped me," Joey said. "Do you have a last name, Caleb?"

"Gunnar," Caleb answered. He had already chosen the name while passing the time riding alone. The name had a nice ring to it.

"If you don't mind me asking, what made you decide to go west at this time in your life?" Joey asked.

Caleb stared into the fire for a moment before answering. "My wife died a couple of years ago and I needed to move on with my life. I couldn't do it there," he said, managing not to lie, but only tell part of the story.

"I'm sorry for your loss. I'm sure that would be a terrible thing to endure," Joey said.

"It was. She died giving birth. We lost our daughter too," Caleb said.

The conversation stopped and they both gazed at the fire and listened to the crackling of the wood as it burned. Neither man seemed able to think of anything else to say.

Finally, Caleb said, "I think I'll call it a day." He crawled into his bedroll and was soon snoring.

Joey sat and watched the fire burn for a while. The flames had him envisioning all the hell that Caroline would raise when she read his telegram. He yawned and decided to turn in for the day.

After breakfast the next morning, the two men headed out again riding Leif. They arrived in Springfield in the mid-morning, riding down the street until they located the telegraph office. Joey composed his telegram and Caleb paid for the message. As they walked out of the office, Caleb handed Joey a twenty-dollar gold piece.

"I'll wait outside while you buy some clothes. There's no need for me to go with you like we're a couple of women," Caleb said.

Joey grinned at him. "You have a point there. Thanks again. I don't know what I would've done without you," he said.

"Just remember that you're going to help me get out west," Caleb said.

"Don't you worry about that. I prefer to have some company," Joey said as he walked to the general store.

Fifteen minutes later, Joey emerged from the store in new trousers, shirt, and suspenders. He carried a new jacket, Caleb's slicker, and a tied brown paper package with another change of clothes.

"You look better," Caleb said.

"Most everybody prefers me with clothes on," Joey joked.

Caleb untied Leif from the hitching rail and they walked towards the livery stable. He didn't like to let the horse out of his sight. The animal was too fine to leave to the temptations of the dishonest.

The blacksmith pounded away at a horseshoe on his anvil as they approached him. He paused in his hammering and asked, "May I help you?"

"I wanted to see what you had in geldings," Joey said.

Distracted by the sight of Leif, the blacksmith couldn't take his eyes off the horse. "That's a fine horse you have there. He's a stallion, isn't he?" he asked.

"He is," Caleb answered.

"I tell you what I'll do. I'll trade you a breeding to my mare for that first gelding there in the corral," the blacksmith said.

Looking the horse over, the animal wasn't deep enough chested and lacked shoulder layback for Caleb's liking. The horse would be fine for pleasure riding, but would never hold up for daily use. "I'd have to see your mare. I don't breed Leif to any old nag," he said.

"Have yourself a look," the blacksmith said as he led the men to a stall inside the stable.

The mare proved to be a fine animal, easily worthy of something that Caleb's daddy would have been proud to own. "She's a fine mare. Are you sure that she's ready? I don't want my horse kicked in the head by some ornery mare that isn't in the mood," Caleb said.

"She's ready. I've had three foals out of her. She'll stand," the blacksmith answered.

Caleb turned and walked out of the stable, giving the blacksmith no choice but to follow. He walked to the corral and studied the horses in it.

"Here's the deal I'll make you," Caleb said. "I'll take that gelding standing in the corner by himself and you throw in a good saddle and bridle for the breeding."

"I can't do that. That's my best gelding. That's too much," the blacksmith said.

"Sure you can. You'll either get a fine mare out of the deal that will produce some fine foals, or if you're lucky, you'll get a stallion that will be nicer than any horse around these parts and people will bring their mares to you and you'll make a killing," Caleb said.

"And I could end up with nothing," the blacksmith complained.

"Well, if that happens, it will be on your mare. I guarantee you that Leif produces. That's the deal. Take it or we'll go elsewhere," Caleb said.

"There is no elsewhere," the blacksmith said.

"There's always an elsewhere," Caleb replied.

The blacksmith looked back and forth between Caleb and Joey. He looked to be taking the measure of the men and whether they would buckle on their demands.

"Oh, all right. You got a deal," the blacksmith said and held out his hand.

Caleb shook with him and then said, "I want to pick out the saddle before we breed them."

The blacksmith looked chagrined. "Come on," he said as he led them to his tack room.

Joey picked out a saddle and bridle to his liking. The blacksmith made his disapproval known by mumbling and sulking.

"Let's get my mare bred before she's out of season while you're fleecing me," the blacksmith groused.

Caleb led Leif to an empty corral and removed his saddle and bridle. The blacksmith led the mare out and the men watched until the breeding was completed. Afterward, Joey saddled his new horse and the two men led their horses away from the livery stable.

"I've known some horse traders in my time, but none of them hold a candle to you. What do I owe you for this?" Joey said.

Smiling, Caleb said, "You can brush Leif out for me tonight. I think he was happy with the arrangement."

"I would say so. The blacksmith not so much," Joey said with a laugh.

They walked to a café and had breakfast before returning to the telegraph office. A telegram authorizing the payment of three hundred dollars waited for them.

"She must think a lot of you to wire you that much money," Caleb said.

"Oh, she does. She needs me, but it doesn't mean that I won't hear about it until the Second Coming. Let's find a gunsmith. With all the money that you saved me, I can get a rifle and revolver," Joey said as they walked to the bank to exchange the note for gold coins.

Joey paid Caleb the money that he owed him and they headed to the gunsmith shop. The shop had the new revolver just like Caleb had purchased and Joey bought it. He also bought a Winchester 73, a scabbard, holster, and cartridges. Some intense negotiations took place before sealing the deal.

As they walked out of the shop, Joey said, "I think it best that we ride out of here after our bartering. Springfield might not take a liking to us."

"Wyoming Territory, here we come," Caleb said as he mounted his horse.

Chapter 5

Caroline Langley rode the buckboard wagon into the yard of the house, not bothering to stop at the barn first to get the ranch hands to help her unload the sacks of feed. She stomped into her home like a five feet four inch whirlwind. As she tossed her Stetson into a chair, the pins holding her hair plastered to her head gave way and her brown hair fell to her shoulders. Claire, her mother, heard the commotion and walked from the kitchen into the parlor.

Upon seeing her daughter's red face and pursed lips, Claire asked, "Caroline, what is it? What's the matter?"

"While I was in town, here comes the telegram messenger with a message from Joey. He got robbed of everything he owned. I had to wire the fool three hundred dollars," Caroline spat out as she used her hands to smooth out her tangled hair.

"Well, I'm sure Joey didn't take any pleasure in getting robbed, dear," Claire said.

"I should have never let him go back home or just fired him," Caroline said.

"Caroline, he hadn't been home in five years. His mother is old and deserved to see her son again," Claire reasoned.

"Joey is more trouble than he's worth. He's like having a little boy working for me," Caroline ranted.

"Shame on you. Joey is the best ranch hand that your father ever hired and you'd be in a world of hurt without him. Look how much extra work you've had to oversee while he's gone," Claire said.

"I knew that you'd take up for him," Caroline protested, cutting her piercing brown eyes towards her mother.

Claire ignored her daughter's glare. "That's because you know I'm right," she said with a smile.

"How will we ever get our money back? These ranch hands couldn't save a penny if their life depended on it," Caroline said.

"Think of it like this - I believe Joey has worked for us for ten years. If you don't get the money back, that comes to thirty dollars a year or two dollars and fifty cents a month. Compared to our other hands, don't you think Joey has been worth an extra two dollars and fifty cents a month?" Claire asked.

Caroline tried not to smile, but her lips curled up in surrender. "Yes, Mother, you are right. You are always right," she said.

Claire smiled back at her daughter. "Of course, I am. That's why I'm the mother and you're the daughter," she teased.

"I need to take the wagon to the barn and get it unloaded," Caroline said and grabbed her hat.

"No, that's not what you need, but I'm too much of a lady to say out loud what that might be," Claire said.

"Mother," Caroline exclaimed.

"Well, it's true. You'll be twenty-seven in a few months and there's more to life than working a ranch all the time. I'm forty-eight and I still miss snuggling up to your father," Claire said.

"Mother, please," Caroline moaned. "Maybe you should take up with Joey. He's not much older than you."

"That could happen. You just never know what a lonely widow is capable of doing and I could do a whole lot worse than Joey Clemson," Claire said.

Truth be told, Claire did miss having Joey on the ranch. He had been a great source of comfort to her after her husband Jackson had been killed by Indians. Joey gave her someone close to her own age to talk with and she always found him a gentleman and a source for reasoned conversation - something that she couldn't always say about her own daughter.

Back in the early years, Claire had worked right beside her husband on the ranch. After they started making money and Caroline had been born, she retired to raising her daughter and running the house. She had taken care of herself over the years and was still a fine looking woman. And regardless of what her daughter thought, she still felt young and not ready to be put out to pasture.

"For goodness sake, Mother, I was only joking. You had Daddy and I had that whoring, good for nothing, scoundrel for a husband. We're done with those things. I'm going to go work and try to forget the last part of this conversation," Caroline said.

"You do that, dear. You can work until you're exhausted, but it still won't scratch that itch," Claire said. She continued laughing after her daughter marched out of the house and slammed the door without saying another word.

Caroline moved the wagon to the barn. Her two ranch hands, Bart and Dan, having just finished cleaning stalls, were standing at the entrance not knowing what next to do. The two men were good workers when given direction, but absolutely useless when left without instructions.

Dan was in his thirties and the smarter of the two men. He knew his way around a horse and was good with the animals. Bart would turn forty during the summer. What he lacked in natural abilities, he made up for with effort, though no one would ever accuse him of making any task easy.

"Let's get the feed unloaded," Caroline barked at them from the seat of the wagon.

Both ranch hands had been hired after the death of Caroline's father and after her husband ran off with another woman. All they had ever seen of Caroline was a demanding, ill-tempered boss, having never known her in happier times. They appreciated the employment and regular pay, but had little affection for their employer. Each grabbed a sack and began stacking the feed.

When's Joey getting back?" Bart asked.

Caroline grabbed a bag and walked towards the barn. The sack of feed weighed nearly half of what she did. With a clenched jaw, she said, "How would I know. I guess when we see him. I'm not his mother." She wasn't about to share the news of the robbery with these two jokers. If Joey wanted them to know, he could tell them himself. She was well aware that her rant with her mother was nothing more than blowing off steam. The ranch would be in a world of hurt if Joey didn't get back soon.

After neatly stacking the feed, Dan asked, "What do you want us to do now?"

"Saddle that gelding that you started calling Diablo. The army would pay top dollar for that horse if we could break him and I plan to do it if it kills me," Caroline said.

"Miss Caroline, that's exactly what's liable to happen. That horse is crazy and you have no business trying to ride him. Let me give it a shot if you're set on breaking him," Dan said.

"No, I aim to take another crack at him. I'm the boss around here," Caroline reminded her ranch hand.

Dan started to speak and then turned to go retrieve the animal. He returned with the horse and led the gelding into the corral. It took both of the ranch hands to hold the horse's head while Caroline tried to mount. The horse continued to step away from the woman, making a circle around the two cowboys as they pivoted with it. Bart moved beside the horse and pushed against its side long enough that Caroline caught up with the animal and climbed into the saddle.

"Let him go, boys," she said and the two men ran for the fence.

Diablo sprang straight up with all four legs in the air and landed stiff legged. He repeated this jump two more times. Caroline felt as if her tailbone had been shoved up to her neck. The horse kicked his rear legs high in the air, giving Caroline a view straight ahead of the ground. On the second buck, she went sailing through the air like a bird in flight and landed in a heap in the dirt. She remained there, stunned, and taking inventory of her body while Bart and Dan came running to her.

"Are you hurt?" Bart asked.

"No," she said as the Dan pulled her to her feet.

"You must have been ten feet in the air," Dan said in astonishment.

"It felt like a long ways coming down. I know that. If I were smart, I'd put a bullet in that horse's hard head," Caroline said, half in admiration and the other in disgust as she eyed her adversary.

Chapter 6

The funeral for Charles Roberts turned into a tense gathering. Britt and her family and friends sat on one side of the church and the Roberts on the other side. Only Charles' mother Hazel seemed cognizant of the fact that her son's behavior led directly to his death. She greeted Britt warmly and gave her a hug while her husband glared at the two of them. The preacher made a point of emphasizing forgiveness in his eulogy to little effect. As the families left the cemetery after the burial, Charles' father and brothers made sure that their threats towards Caleb could be heard as they climbed into their buggies.

Sheriff Briar and his deputies had spent the three days after finding Charles' body trying to track Caleb. They gave up never having figured out which direction he departed or finding a single person that had seen him leave. In frustration, the Roberts family put up a thousand dollar reward and the sheriff had a wanted poster printed and distributed. The lawman had no other plans to find Caleb but to wait to see if the posters provided any leads.

Albert Roberts and his two sons paid a visit to the jail. They caught the sheriff drinking coffee with his feet up on his desk and reading the newspaper. The sheriff hastily put his feet on the floor and folded up the paper.

"Albert, what brings you to town?" Sheriff Briar asked.

"I came to see if you were doing anything to find Caleb. I guess I already have my answer to that," Albert answered in irritated voice.

"I don't know what else I can do besides wait to see if the posters bring us some information," the sheriff said.

"You could go talk to Nils again and this time lean on him. You know damn well that they know more than they're telling," Albert said.

"That may be true, but you wouldn't give up one of your sons to the law and they won't either," Sheriff Briar said.

"You know I hold a lot of sway in this county. If you want to get reelected, I suggest you get off your ass and try to find my son's killer," Albert said before turning and walking out of the jail.

The sheriff eased himself out of his chair and retrieved his hat from his desk. He ambled outside and gave his horse a disgusted look before mounting the animal. With a sigh that betrayed his lack of enthusiasm for the task at hand, he headed towards the Berg farm. He found Nils Berg watering his beds of tobacco seedlings. Nils walked over to the sheriff as the lawman climbed down from his horse.

"Sheriff Briar, what brings you out this way?" Nils inquired.

"Nils, I need to talk to you about Caleb again. The Roberts clan is giving me trouble. They want some answers. Do you know where Caleb is?" Sheriff Briar asked.

"I lie awake at night worrying about Caleb and where he is? I tell you that I have no idea of my son's whereabouts," Nils answered.

"Do you know which way he headed?" the sheriff persisted.

"I never saw my son after he left here that Friday evening. I believe Charles was most likely still alive at that point and that Caleb had no intention of killing him. Caleb is a fine son and a good person. I still believe that Charles gave Caleb no choice but to defend himself," Nils replied.

"That may well be, but he shouldn't have run. If you hear from Caleb, you need to let me know. Otherwise, you are aiding and abetting a fugitive and you'll be in trouble too," the sheriff said, giving Nils a hard look.

Nils met the sheriff's stare head on. "I'll do that," he said with a touch of sarcasm.

The sheriff averted his eyes before climbing onto his horse and riding away without saying another word. He rode straight to Albert Roberts' home and found him in his barn tending to his horses.

"I went to talk to Nils. If he knows anything, he's not talking, and to be honest, I really don't think he has a clue to Caleb's whereabouts. We'll just have to hope that somebody recognizes Caleb from the poster," Sheriff Briar said.

"You couldn't find your ass if it wasn't fastened on. Get out of here. You're useless," Albert said and turned his back to continue feeding his horses until the sheriff rode away.

Albert saddled up his horse and walked the animal over to a shed where his two sons were changing shares on their plows in anticipation of starting to work the fields.

"Get on your horses. We're going to take a ride to the Berg place. That sorry sheriff can't get any answers, but I bet by God we can," Albert said.

The two brothers grinned at their father before retrieving their horses. The Berg home sat only three miles away and the father and two sons rode at an easy trot to their destination.

Nils was putting his stallions in the barn for the night when he saw the Roberts family riding up the driveway. He hurriedly put the last horse up and waited in front of the barn. The Roberts clan didn't scare Nils, but he anticipated an unpleasant visit.

"Albert, what brings you out this way?" Nils asked as the men stopped in front of him.

Albert didn't speak until he and sons had climbed off their horses. "Nils, you might be able to pull one over on that sheriff, but I'll not have it. I want to know where Caleb is," he said.

"Like I told Sheriff Briar, I never saw Caleb again after he left here on Friday evening. I believe he never stopped to say goodbye so that he wouldn't involve us. I'm telling you that I do not have a clue to his whereabouts," Nils said in a measured tone.

"Do you really expect me to believe that?" Albert asked.

"I don't really care what you believe or don't believe. Now you need to get off my property," Nils said.

Michael, the eldest son, grabbed Nils by the shirt and yanked him until their faces were practically touching. "And what are you going to do about it if we don't? Do you think that useless sheriff would help you? Now tell us where Caleb is or we will beat it out of you," he said.

Olivia watched the men from her kitchen window. When she saw Michael grab her husband, she calmly walked to the outside door and retrieved the shotgun above it. She checked the loads and then walked out onto the porch. As she pulled the hammers back on both barrels, she started marching towards the men. "I don't know if Caleb did or didn't have the mettle to kill Charles, but I swear to you if you don't leave right now, that I do. If you don't leave Britt and us alone, we'll contact U.S. Marshal Lucien Eaton. Nils sold him a horse last year. I'm sure that he would be more than happy to come help us. We received a letter from him about a month ago telling us his horse is the best mount he has ever owned," she said and raised the shotgun up to her shoulder.

"Olivia, be careful. That gun has touchy triggers," Nils called out.

"Good," Olivia replied.

Michael released Nils and stepped back.

"Come on boys. Let's get out of here," Albert said.

After the Roberts rode away, Nils grinned as he walked over to his wife and took the shotgun from her. He released the triggers and gently returned the hammers before putting his arm around his wife. "You even had me believing you knew what you were doing," he said.

"I did know what I was doing and I wasn't playing either. That family is nothing but trouble," Olivia said.

"I won't argue with you there," he said.

"Maybe we should have convinced Caleb to stay and contacted Marshal Eaton," Olivia said.

"Truth be told, I never thought of that. I doubt he would have stopped a grand jury from taking it to trial anyway and he certainly wouldn't have had any sway over a jury convicting Caleb," Nils said.

"Do you think today will be the end of it?" she asked.

"I don't know. The Roberts have more money than sense," Nils said as he walked his wife into their home.

Chapter 7

Three days after leaving Springfield, Caleb and Joey camped for the night outside of Independence, Missouri. They rode into town in the morning and bought supplies before leaving on the Oregon Trail. With the completion of the Pacific Railroad in 1869, the trail's popularity had waned, but still found some traffic for pioneers heading west to find their fortunes.

"How come you just didn't take the train back home?" Caleb asked as they passed by Shawnee Mission.

"I don't know. I just like wide-open space and I figured this would be my last time to ride. I'll probably take the train the next time whenever that will be. What about you?" Joey said.

"I didn't know where I was going. I guess I just figured I'd know it when I rode there," Caleb answered.

By late afternoon, they reached Gardner, Kansas. Joey pointed towards the southwest. "That way is the Santa Fe Trail. This here is the divide between it and the Oregon Trail. This is your last chance to change course," he said.

"I think I'll stay with you. I'd rather keep the company of a Yankee than go out on my own and get lost," Caleb said.

Joey smiled. "That's fine with me as long as I don't have to hear too many 'you-all' and 'fixing to' along the way," he said.

"I'm told that Yankee women love a southern drawl," Caleb joked.

"Well, if you haven't noticed, I'm not a woman. And I find that slow talking, dragging out a sentence, just plain old annoying," Joey said.

Caleb grinned. "The next time that I see somebody walking in their underwear, I'm fixing to tell them real quick that I'm not interested in helping. I'll just say you-all are on your own," he said.

The two men rode for another couple of hours before making camp for the night. They arose early the next day and made it to the Wakarusa River by mid-morning. Crossing the stream by bridge at Blue Jacket, Joey informed Caleb that the spot was named for a family that had once run a ferry there. He also reminisced of his first trip out west with a wagon train before the ferry existed and having to dismantle and lower the wagons down the limestone rocks before towing them across the river and pulling them up the other bank.

In early afternoon, they reached the little town of Tecumseh. The village appeared to be dying. Several buildings were boarded up and looked in disrepair. As they passed by a trading post with four horses tied outside, Joey pulled his horse up abruptly.

Pointing with his finger, Joey said, "That's my horse and I recognize that bay from the robbers."

Caleb rubbed the back of his neck with his hand. "What do you want to do?" he asked, dreading the answer he thought he'd hear.

"I'm going in there to confront them and take my horse back. They won't be so cocky this time," Joey said.

"They may live here and we'll have the whole town after us," Caleb warned.

"You can ride on and I'll catch up with you if things turn out my way. This isn't your fight," Joey said.

"Oh, it is. "I'm not about to run out on you now," Caleb said.

"I appreciate your loyalty. If this gets ugly, just remember smooth and steady beats fast and wild. I knew a gunman back in the day and he always said that you didn't have to be fast, just faster and more accurate than the other guy. He said most shooters rush their shot. One time, a man drawing on him missed his gun completely. The only thing pointing at my friend turned out to be the man's finger - a fatal mistake," Joey said.

They tied the horses to the hitching rail and walked into the store. The front room looked crammed with the usual goods that customers sought, and the clerk could barely be seen behind the counter stacked high with merchandise. A dirty curtain hung in the doorway to another room. Joey led the way through the curtain into the back. Caleb stood to the left of Joey, nearest the bar. The room was poorly lit, filled with smoke, and smelled of beer. Three men sat at a table next to the wall playing cards, smoking stogies, and drinking beer. The robbers never noticed the new arrivals.

Caleb sized up the three men. Two of them were large and broad in the shoulder, probably brothers. The other man looked small and wiry. They were all dirty and wore clothes that had seen better days. None of them looked like somebody that you would invite over for Sunday dinner.

"Can I help you?" the man behind the bar asked.

"I'm here to see those men," Joey said loudly.

The three men looked up from their card game.

"I came to take my horse back. Keep your hands where I can see them," Joey said in a measured tone.

The man in middle of the three smiled. "You should just be happy that we left you alive. If we hadn't robbed you, you wouldn't be wearing all those new clothes there, now would you?" he said.

The bartender began to slowly reach under the counter.

Caleb looked towards the bar. "Mister, this doesn't concern you. If I were you, I'd rest my hands on your bar where everybody can see them. It would be a shame to get mixed up in these three thieves' affairs," he said. The bartender complied with the request.

Joey took a step towards the table. "You men can strip off your clothes. I aim to return the favor and leave you in your underwear," he said.

The man in the middle cut his eyes to the right to make eye contact with his companion and then repeated the motion to his left before flipping over the table. As the three outlaws rose to their feet, Joey and Caleb drew their revolvers. The outlaws reached for their pistols, but before their guns cleared the holsters, Joey and Caleb began shooting. Caleb fired two shots into the man farthest to his left and Joey did likewise to the outlaw on the right. Both men were driven back into the wall by the impact of the shots fired at close range. The thief that had done all the talking had cleared leather and was bringing his gun up as Caleb and Joey fired a barrage of four bullets into him. As the shots drove the outlaw back against the wall, he sent a round into the ceiling of the saloon. The three men sat with their backs to the wall as if passing time, but all had passed from life. A cloud of black powder smoke filled the small room to the point that breathing became a chore. In the haze, the bartender stood with his trembling hands in the air.

"Did you know those men?" Joey asked the bartender.

The bartender shook his head. "I've never seen them before today," he said.

"You heard them admit that they robbed me and you saw them go for their guns. Are you going to tell the truth when the law comes?" Joey asked.

"I don't have a reason to lie, but I'd prefer you take your business elsewhere the next time you come to town," the bartender said in a haughty voice.

"On that you have my word," Joey said as they walked through the doorway into the front room to get some fresh air.

The bartender sent word for the constable to come. The peace officer walked into the trading post looking more like a farmer than the law with his flop hat and bib overalls that needed a good washing. He seemed to have an aversion to the dead and stayed well away from the bodies. Looking over at the bartender, he said, "So, what happened here?"

Clearing his throat before speaking, the bartender gave an accurate accounting of the encounter.

The constable eyed Joey and Caleb with a contemptuous expression. "The town will have to bury those men. You could have killed them somewhere else. You boys need to leave and not come back," he said.

"We're riding out of here with the horse that they stole from me. Don't worry, we're planning on moving on and won't be back," Joey said.

"The town will take possession of the rest of their belongings. Go on and get," the constable said.

The two men made a hasty retreat outdoors. Joey grabbed the reins to his old horse before mounting the one they had bartered for at the livery stable. He and Caleb put the horses into a lope all the way to the Kansas River where they slowed to a walk as they crossed the bridge.

"Do you think that's the end of this?" Caleb asked. "I'm still shaking."

"I think so, but I don't plan to hang around to find out. That constable didn't strike me as someone that would make much effort to look for us if he had a change of heart," Joey said.

Caleb fought the urge to stop and vomit. His stomach rolled and his nerves were shot. Except for the war, he had managed to live his life without shooting anybody and now in a little over a week he had killed twice. Even though the shootings were justified, he wondered what his life had turned into now. "I wouldn't want to make a habit of that. Have you ever killed besides the war?" he asked.

"I have. The Wyoming Territory is not as civilized as back east. I've been in Indian battles and dealt with rustlers. We hang rustlers on the spot. Thank you for sticking with me. I know that wasn't easy for you," Joey said.

They pushed the horses as hard as they dared knowing of the long journey still ahead of them. The land appeared mostly flat with a road well used that made for easy travel. After covering a good distance through the afternoon, they made camp past Rossville, Kansas.

Once they finished their evening meal, Caleb said, "Killing a man is a heck of a thing, isn't it? Even during the war, and all that bloodshed, I never got used to it."

"It is and I hope I never do get used to killing. I take no pleasure in it, but some people are best dead," Joey said.

"Did you plan on killing those men today?" Caleb asked.

"I wouldn't say that I planned it, but I figured as much. They didn't strike me as men that would like to give things back," Joey answered.

Caleb picked up a twig and tossed it into the fire. He watched it burn. His conscience got the better of him and he needed to unburden himself. "I didn't tell you the whole story about me leaving home. My brother-in-law beat my sister and I went over to their place to give him a licking. He started shooting at me and I had to kill him. His family pretty much controls the town and I knew that I'd never get a fair trial. I didn't cotton to hanging for defending myself," Caleb said.

"I figured you were on the run. Even with losing your wife, you didn't strike me as somebody that would just pull up stakes and head out west," Joey said.

"Are you okay with that?" Caleb asked.

"I am. I'd be some kind of fool to turn my back on you now after all you've done for me. Your secret is safe," Joey said.

"I appreciate that. I feel better not having such a secret between us," Caleb said.

"Caleb, I credit myself with being a pretty fair judge of character. Don't be so hard on yourself. You're a good man. A man that beats his wife needs a good killing anyways," Joey said.

With a sad smile, Caleb said, "I sure do miss my family though. We're a close bunch and we were together all the time. I might not ever see them again."

"I understand. That's why I went home to visit my mom," Joey said.

"Have you ever been married, Joey?" Caleb asked.

"Nah, it's hard to keep a wife on a ranch hand's salary and I like being a cowboy too much to probably ever change now," Joey answered.

"My wife's name was Robin. We had a good marriage and a lot of good times," Caleb reminisced.

"Caleb, I'm really sorry that you lost her. I know it has to be hard," Joey said.

"I don't have the words to tell you how much losing someone so young and full of life hurts. And that precious little baby – we planned on calling her Amanda. That much loss changes a man," Caleb said before jumping up to gather wood to throw on the fire. With his back turned, he made a quick swipe of his sleeve across his eyes.

When Caleb returned, he decided to change the subject to something less sorrowful. The two men talked and debated the things they liked in a good horse for the rest of the evening before turning in for the night.

Chapter 8

The absence of Joey Clemson around the haunts of Fort Laramie had not gone unnoticed by the local citizenry. Every time that Bart and Dan ventured to the Fort Laramie Saloon, somebody would ask about Joey's whereabouts. The two ranch hands had explained his trip back home to Illinois to see his mother so many times that they were tired of the subject and longed for Joey's return. Nonetheless, the rumor got started that Joey had a parting of ways with Caroline Langley and would not be returning to the Langley ranch.

The cattle ranchers in the area had always taken a dim view of the wild mustangs that ran on the free range. Horses were much harder on the grass than cattle and the ranchers constantly complained about the animals stunting the grazing land. Caroline's father, Jackson Langley, had garnered enough respect and sway in the community to keep the cattle rancher's from acting out on their dislike of the wild horses. After Jackson's death, Joey's presence on the Langley ranch had been enough to keep the rancher's in check.

Every spring, Caroline and the rest of the crew would drive as many of the wild horses to the ranch as they could find. The colts that had matured enough that the knee joints had closed were shepherded into one fenced pasture to begin training. Brood mares were pastured in another. They would then release the wild stallions and the young and too old horses. Pandemonium would ensue on the ranch for a few days until the wild stallions and the yearlings gave up on reaching the mares and returned to the range. The mares were kept pastured together while they foaled. At that point, the ranch's stallions were turned out with the mares to breed during the foal heat. This practice began when Jackson Langley first started ranching and had worked so well that they were the army's preferred supplier of horses to the fort.

Caroline walked to the bunkhouse. Bart and Dan were cleaning up their breakfast dishes when she entered.

"I want you two to go out today and scout where the mustangs are staying. If Joey isn't back soon, we'll have to begin rounding them up without him. We need to begin preparing," Caroline said.

"Everybody thinks Joey isn't coming back. I'm beginning to wonder myself," Bart said.

"People just like to talk and make up stories. I got a telegram from him and he's on his way. He needs to catch the train at Cheyenne if he ever goes back again. This isn't the old days," Caroline said and walked out of the bunkhouse.

Bart and Dan rode up into the foothills to the valleys where the horses tended to gather in the spring with the greening of the grass. The first two dells they stopped at had cattle from the other area ranches. As they topped a ridge overlooking the third valley on their trek, they pulled their horses up hard and stared down below them. Dan held up his hand and pointed with his finger as he counted. Fifteen horses lay dead down below them. Buzzards stood on the horse's ribcages and tore junks of flesh from the bodies. The stench of the rotting carcasses drifted up out of the valley and forced Bart to turn his horse and retreat before he lost his breakfast.

Dan pulled his Winchester from the scabbard and took aim on a buzzard. Exhaling slowly, he gently squeezed the trigger. As the roar of the shot echoed in the valley, one of the birds collapsed off the ribcage of a horse and onto the ground. The sound of beating wings filled the air as the rest of the buzzards took flight. Dan pulled a kerchief from his pocket and wadded up the material. He held it against his nose and mouth as he rode into the valley.

Most of the horses were too mutilated by the birds to determine a cause of death, but Dan found two of the animals that clearly had a bullet hole in the skull. Not wishing to linger in the putrid surroundings, he heeled his horse into a trot out of the valley back to where he found Bart.

"They were shot," Dan said.

"I figured as much. Caroline is going to be fit to be tied when she finds out what happened," Bart said.

"I guess I'll get the pleasure of telling her. It'll probably be our fault somehow anyway," Dan said.

After returning to the ranch, Dan found Caroline in the tack room vigorously rubbing neatsfoot oil into her saddle. She looked up at him as he entered the room with her usual dour expression as if she assumed he had already done something that would displease her.

"What is it?" Caroline asked brusquely.

"We found fifteen mustangs dead. They looked to have been shot. They've been dead awhile and the buzzards have worked them over pretty good, but I think it was that old stallion we called Trooper and his band of mares and yearlings," Dan replied.

Caroline tossed her rag onto the saddle. She spun around, marched to the wall, turned back, and returned. "This is what I get for letting Joey be gone all winter. The cattle ranchers are going to try to kill off the mustang herds. They think with my daddy dead and Joey gone that they can finally have all the land for their cattle. I wonder which rancher killed the horses," she said.

"I wouldn't be surprised if Sanders, Rhodes, and Horn aren't all in on it. Those three ranchers have the most to gain from wiping out the herds and they've all made their voices heard around town of their low opinions of wild horses," Dan said.

Looking at her ranch hand, Caroline decided that Dan could very well be right. She tended to think of him and Bart as being dense as a heavy fog, but truth be told, Dan had a pretty good head on his shoulders whenever he decided to clear the cobwebs and dust from it.

"That's quite possible. Do you think any of their ranch hands might get to bragging in the saloons?" Caroline asked.

"It's possible. Cowboys like to jaw after a couple of beers. One of them might start blustering about killing the horses," Dan replied.

"If you'd be so inclined, I'd give you a Half Eagle to take Bart to town to see if the two of you can learn anything at the saloons," Caroline said.

Dan smiled. "I'm not about to turn down a free night in town," he said.

"Good. Walk with me to the house. I'm going to grab a jacket and then ride to all three ranches. Loren Sanders, Thomas Rhodes, and Nathan Horn are going to learn that they are in for a fight if they think they are going to put us under," Caroline said.

"I better go with you, Miss Caroline," Dan said.

Caroline pulled her head back and put her hands on her hips. "Do I look as if I need a babysitter to you? I'm quite capable of taking care of myself. None of those men are man enough to tangle with me in person," she said in a slightly shrill voice.

Dan looked at Caroline and realized that the bond he had felt with her a moment before had been as fleeting as a snowflake in hell. In his opinion, the woman was insufferable and a bane to her sex.

"Yes, ma'am," Dan said.

"Don't call me ma'am. I am not old. You and Bart need to spend the rest of the day making sure the fences are ready for the mustangs. We had better start rounding them up tomorrow. Come with me," Caroline said before heading for the door.

Walking back to her home as if she were on a march, Caroline slipped inside, leaving Dan standing on the porch. She quietly retrieved the five-dollar piece and grabbed her coat on the way out the door.

"You'll be the only one that knows where I'm going. I should be back before you head to town," Caroline said as she handed Dan the coin.

"I'll make sure that you are before we leave," Dan promised as he walked with his employer back to the barn.

Caroline retrieved a spare saddle from the tack room, leaving her half-cleaned one to be finished later. Her personal horse was an eight-year-old sorrel gelding with flaxen mane and tail that stood fourteen and one-half hands. The horse had been foaled by a mustang mare and one of the ranch's stallions. Caroline had grown attached to the animal when they were breaking him to ride and had sweet-talked her father into letting her have him. Buddy had been her everyday horse since that time. She saddled him and headed towards Loren Sanders' place.

The three ranches that Caroline suspected might be involved in the killing of the horses were spread in an arc to the north of the Langley ranch while Fort Laramie lay to the south. The Sanders ranch sat farthest to the west of the three and Caroline put Buddy into a lope as she headed there. The horse liked to run and she had to rein him in to keep the animal from breaking into a gallop. Caroline locked into the rhythm of her mount and relaxed. She loved to ride and ride fast. If the reason for her travel hadn't been so dire, she would have thoroughly enjoyed the day. Buddy worked up a lather as they traveled and Caroline slowed him to a walk for the last half-mile of the journey to the ranch.

Loren Sanders stood in the barnyard supervising his ranch hands while they replaced a wheel on a buckboard wagon as Caroline rode up to the men.

Looking up, Loren said, "Caroline, what a surprise. What brings you out here?"

"I wanted to have a word with you alone if that is possible," Caroline said.

"Certainly. Let's go inside the house," Loren said as he took the reins from Caroline and passed the horse off to one of his ranch hands before escorting the young woman to the house.

Inside the home, Loren led Caroline to an office off the entrance. He shut the door and waited for her to take a seat before sitting down at the desk.

"What can I do for you?" Loren asked.

"Dan and Bart found fifteen dead mustangs that had been shot. I wanted to know if you knew anything about it," Caroline stated.

Caroline's father had always maintained a civil and working relationship with the other three ranchers. He liked to say that Loren played his cards close to the vest and kept a poker face as he did so. Loren also had the ability to tell a person what they wanted to hear whether he agreed with them or had any intention of keeping a promise he made.

"In other words you are asking me if I'm responsible for the deaths of those animals and the answer is no. I've never made any secret of my distaste for the mustangs to your father or anybody else, but I wouldn't be a party to ruining my neighbor's livelihood either," Loren said.

Studying the rancher, Caroline tried to determine if he had spoken the truth. She wasn't sure, but decided that if he were a liar, he was a good one.

"Just so you know, I will not stand by and let what my father worked so hard to achieve be destroyed without a fight," Caroline said.

"I wouldn't expect otherwise, but I'm not your problem," Loren said.

Standing, Caroline held out her hand and shook with the rancher. "Thank you for your time, Mr. Sanders," she said.

They walked back to the barn where Caroline departed with a wave. She headed northeast towards the Rhodes ranch. With the friskiness run off her horse, she put him into an easy trot. As the young woman rode, she thought about Thomas Rhodes. She expected this meeting not to be as pleasant as the one with Loren Sanders. Thomas was known for his obnoxious behavior and the flaunting of his wealth. He also had a reputation as a womanizer.

Caroline rode up the driveway to the ranch, but didn't see anybody outside. She tied her horse to a brass horsehead hitching post, walked to the front door, and knocked. Mrs. Rhodes greeted her.

"Caroline Langley, what a surprise. Come on in. What brings you out this way?" Mrs. Rhodes said.

"I was hoping to talk to Mr. Rhodes," Caroline replied.

"He's in his study. Come with me. How is Claire?" Mrs. Rhodes asked as she took off down a hall.

"She is fine and as feisty as ever," Caroline answered.

"Thomas, you have company," Mrs. Rhodes said as she led Caroline into the room and shut the door as she departed.

The study proved to be an impressive display of wealth with its walnut desk trimmed in brass and bookcases to the ceiling filled with leather bound books. Carpet overlaid the floor and high-grade leather covered each chair.

"Caroline, it's been a long time since I've seen you. What can I do for you?" Thomas asked before taking a puff on an enormous Cuban cigar and exhaling into the already smoke laden air.

"My ranch hands found fifteen mustangs shot dead. I want to know if you are behind the killings," Caroline said, deciding to forego any niceties over the situation.

Thomas smiled at her with the cigar clamped between his teeth as his beady eyes twinkled while studying the young woman's figure. "Can't say I know anything about that. You and Claire need to sell that place and get out of the horse business anyway. Move to town and find you a man to take care of a pretty little thing like yourself. You come to me first when you want to sell. I'll make you a generous offer," he said.

Caroline had to make a herculean effort to keep from showing the anger she felt. She could feel color coming to her face in spite of her struggle to remain calm. In a voice more emotional than she intended, she said. "Mother and I will die fighting to preserve what Daddy built. Anybody that thinks they can run us off will find themselves at war."

"I've always admired your spunk, Caroline. If you were born a man, I believe you would run this here county, but unfortunately for you, you were born the fairer sex. Regardless, I am not the source of your grievance. You're wasting your and my time," Thomas said.

Standing, Caroline walked out of the room without saying goodbye and let herself out of the house. She climbed on Buddy and took off in a fast lope until she covered some distance from the home. As she slowed the horse to a trot, she shuddered and felt as if she needed to go home to take a bath. She despised men that treated women as mere objects put on this earth for their pleasure.

As she crossed some open range land, Caroline came across a cattle herd. Nathan Horn, his son, Milo, and a couple of their ranch hands sat on their horses on a hill overlooking the animals. She trotted up to the men and stopped.

Milo had been sweet on her back in school, but she had always considered him too vain and in love with his daddy's money to be a fitting suitor. He hadn't taken the rejection well and had persisted in his attempts to woo her until she had been forced to humiliate him in front of the class to make him stop. Milo had never spoken to her since that day.

"Hello, Mr. Horn," Caroline said.

"Caroline," Nathan greeted her. "What are you doing over here?"

Once again, she told of the dead horses and asked the ranch owner if he knew anything of it. She could see that she had rancored Nathan before she even finished talking.

"Little lady, I'm not in the habit of being accused of malicious behavior. Those damn horses have been nothing but a detriment to all of us trying to make a living raising cattle. I didn't have anything to do with killing those mustangs, but if I were to take a notion to, I sure wouldn't need yours or anybody else's permission. I'll tend to my cattle and I suggest you go play with your horses while they are still living. I'm done with this conversation," Nathan said and nudged his horse into a walk.

Caroline sat there for a moment as the four men rode down the hill towards the cattle with their backs to her. She turned Buddy and kicked him into a gallop. Her Daddy had always said that a rattlesnake wouldn't mess with Nathan Horn on a bad day and she now believed it.

She wanted to cry, but wouldn't allow herself such a weakness. Her whole day had been wasted on folly. The idea that one of the three ranchers would come right out and admit to killing the mustangs now seemed absurd. Words were a waste of time. Only action would save the horses and the ranch. As her eyes welled with tears, she swore on her daddy's grave that she would save both of them or die trying.

Chapter 9

Caleb and Joey had spent the previous day covering as much ground as their horses could tolerate. They had passed what once had been St. Mary's Mission where Jesuit priests had taught Potawatomi children, but had just reopened that year as a men's college. Afterwards, they crossed rivers at Red Vermillion Crossing and Black Vermillion Crossing before making camp for the night. Joey had been like a history teacher with all his reminiscing about past trips when wagons had to ford the rivers before the ferries started making the crossings a much easier proposition.

In the morning, the two men arose early and ate breakfast, hitting the trail just as the sun broke above the horizon. An hour and a half later, they came upon Alcove Spring with its waterfall rushing out of the rocks into a pool of water. Lush vegetation surrounded the spot.

"Back in this trail's heyday, this spot would have families picnicking all over it. It made for a nice break from the travel. I met Ann Stahl here. She was this pretty little eighteen year old traveling with her German immigrant family. She spoke broken English, but my heart sure heard her. I still think about her sometimes and wonder what happened to her," Joey said, smiling at the memory.

"Ah, so you're a romantic at heart and still remember her name after all these years," Caleb said.

"I wouldn't say there's much romantic about a man that's spent most of his life living in a bunkhouse. Kind of sad really," Joey said.

"You're not dead yet. They say the older the violin, the sweeter the music. Maybe you're getting ready to cut loose with a symphony," Caleb teased.

"I doubt that. I'd have intentions on Caroline's mother, Claire, if I had a higher station in life. I don't think she'd be interested in the hired help, but she's a fine looking woman and as sweet as candy. Caroline would probably fire me or kill me, or knowing her, something worse - if you know what I mean," Joey said and grinned.

"That sounds like it could make for a complicated situation. You sure make it sound as if there's no pleasure in working for Caroline," Caleb said.

"Oh, don't get me wrong. She's a good person and will do right by you, but life has stomped all the joy out of her. Losing her daddy was hard on her. They were close. Her no count husband stole whatever happiness that her daddy's death hadn't already robbed from her. I still have hopes that someday she'll get back to being her old self," Joey said.

"I don't think I'll ever get over the death of Robin and the baby. I fear that some changes are forever," Caleb said.

The two men fell silent and didn't speak again until they reached the Big Blue River. Joey knew where to cross the stream and they made it to the other side without having to make the horses swim.

Clear skies allowed the sun to warm the air, making for pleasant travel and allowing the men to shed their coats. They had ridden about a mile from the river when a rider emerged out of a tree line from the northeast. The bareheaded man approached them with his horse at a trot. As he neared, they could see that he was a boy of probably no more than eighteen. He slowed his horse to a walk as he rode up beside Caleb. The boy's horse was drenched in lather and its sides heaved as the animal snorted air.

Smiling, the kid said, "Good morning. I was wondering if I could ride with you a spell. My pa don't like me riding alone."

Looking down at the boy's horse, Caleb said, "I don't know. It looks as if you are in a considerable bigger hurry than we are. What's your name?"

"My name is Roger. I just needed to stretch my horse out this morning," the boy said.

"Well, Roger, your horse must need an awful lot of stretching," Caleb said.

Joey leaned around Caleb to get a better look at Roger. "Where're you headed?" he asked.

"Fort Kearny," Roger replied.

"Considering that you're not carrying a gun or saddlebags, you are traveling a little light for a multiday trip," Joey said.

"I've had a run of bad luck. Had to sell whatever I owned," Roger said.

Caleb turned his head and made eye contact with Joey. His riding partner looked as doubtful about Roger's story as he felt. Joey shrugged his shoulders.

While looking back at Roger, Caleb said, "You can ride with us until your horse cools and then you need to be riding on. I can see trouble all over you and we don't have time for it."

"Fair enough," Roger said.

They rode at a walk for the next half-hour. Roger kept looking over his shoulder and seemed to get more nervous the longer they traveled.

"Are you expecting someone?" Caleb asked Roger when the boy turned to look over his shoulder again.

"Oh, damn, they're coming," Roger said and kicked his horse into a run.

"Wait ..." Caleb yelled before turning to see four riders coming at a hard lope.

Caleb and Joey turned their horses towards the advancing men and rested their hands on their revolvers. All four riders kept both their hands on the reins as they neared. Two of the men rode on past after Roger and the others pulled up in front of Caleb and Joey.

"You were riding with a horse thief," one of men said.

"We'd never before seen him until a little while ago. I expect you saw the tracks where he rode up on us and asked if he could ride along," Caleb said.

"I did. Still don't mean you aren't partners," the man said.

"I don't appreciate being accused of associating with horse thieves. My partner and I come from horse ranches. We aren't exactly partial to people that steal horses. Seeing as how we came from a different direction than the boy, I don't know how you think we timed all this up. And besides, we have an extra horse. If we knew him, it would have made a lot more sense to ride to him with a good horse instead of having him steal that old nag. We're headed to Fort Laramie and that horse would never make it," Caleb said in a lecturing voice.

The man sat on his horse and seemed to be contemplating what Caleb had said. He finally rubbed his chin and said, "I suppose you have some valid points."

"They got him," the other man said.

One of the others had Roger lassoed and was returning fast enough that the boy had to run to keep from being yanked off his feet. The second rider followed with the stolen horse in tow.

As the rider leading Roger neared, the man that had done all the talking, said, "There's some big cottonwood trees over there near the river. We can hang him there."

"You don't want to do that. He's just a boy," Caleb said.

"We don't have any choice. You wouldn't let your ranch get a reputation for allowing horse stealing and we can't either. And if he steals once, he's likely to steal again," the man said.

"If he doesn't learn horseflesh and how not to bake a horse, he'll get caught again and they can hang him," Caleb said, trying to lighten the mood.

"I take no pleasure in this. It's just the way things are," the man said.

"Don't you have a lawman around here somewhere that you can take the boy?" Caleb asked.

"Some things we just handle ourselves," the man said. "The law understands."

Placing his hand back onto his revolver, Caleb said, "I don't think I can let you do that."

Joey moved his horse up a step and grasped Caleb's arm. "Caleb, this isn't our concern. I know that where you come from that the law would handle this, but out here, things are different. People have to protect what is theirs. We need to go," he said.

Caleb looked over at Roger. The boy's shoulders shuddered as tears ran down his dusty cheeks. He looked pitiful and even younger than his age.

"But Joey, he's just a boy," Caleb pleaded.

"He's old enough to know what happens if you steal a horse and get caught. Come on," Joey said with authority.

Turning his horse, Joey nudged the animal into a walk and Caleb followed suit. Caleb looked back once and saw the four men leading Roger towards the tree line along the river.

"Joey, I still think we should do something," Caleb said.

"We'd have to kill four men that were just protecting their property to save a horse thief. Surely, you've heard of hanging horse thieves in Tennessee," Joey said.

"Of course I've heard of it, and in Tennessee too, but I sure never witnessed it before now. My family never had any horses stolen and I still think it's a matter for the law to handle," Caleb said.

"In a perfect world that would be true, but you need to understand that the farther west we travel, the more imperfect things become. Where we're headed, a man has to protect what's his or suffer the consequences. You need to get used to that," Joey said.

"I do understand. I wouldn't be riding with you right now if I hadn't tried to protect my sister. I just don't cotton to hanging a boy," Caleb said.

"We need to get to moving and make up some lost time. If we don't get back to Fort Laramie before long, you're liable to be protecting me from Caroline," Joey said before nudging his horse into a lope.

The two men pushed on into Nebraska and Joey insisted that they make it to Rock Creek Station before calling it a day. The station had originally been built as a stop on the Pony Express, but now served as a trading post. Joey had resumed riding his original horse and they decided to use the horse they had bartered for to tote supplies. The clerk gave them some empty feed sacks to use to carry the bacon, salt pork, and other supplies they purchased and they hung their goods from the saddle of the extra horse before making camp west of the post.

Joey noticed Caleb's lack of appetite and dearth of conversation. As Caleb was wont to do, he was staring into the fire and looking as if his mind was a million miles away. A pained expression on his face revealed the hurt he carried inside of him like a cancer. Joey had seen Caleb do the same thing on the trail when the young man would go for hours without talking or even seem to be cognizant that he had a riding partner.

"Are you going to be all right?" Joey asked.

"I'll be fine. I was sitting here thinking that I've seen more death in the last couple of weeks than I had the whole time since the war. It seems to be following me," Caleb said.

"Ah, things will get better. Today was one of those deals where if we'd been an hour earlier or later, we would have never known what was going on. Just bad timing," Joey said.

"I hope things do get better. Doesn't seem like you or I have been having much luck lately," Caleb said before looking down at his wrist and noticing the bracelet that the old woman had given him in Missouri. Alice's words about not letting tragedy be his view of the world came back to him. As he rubbed the bracelet with his fingers, he looked at Joey and smiled sadly. "To better days," he said.

Chapter 10

The trip that Dan and Bart made to town to try to learn some information on the horse killings had proved fruitless. After that, two days of spring rains had put the mustang roundup on hold. The downpours had left everything a soggy mess. Late in the afternoon of the second day, the sky cleared and the sun emerged. Caroline saddled Buddy and headed for town. After being cooped up in the house watching it rain, she enjoyed the escape from the ranch and the fresh smelling air. The sandy loam soil in the area drained well and the horse had little trouble finding good footing on the road into Fort Laramie.

Caroline tied the horse at the hitching rail in front of the Fort Laramie Saloon and walked into the establishment. She always enjoyed the slight audible gasp from the patrons when they saw a woman other than the saloon girls entering their domain. The place would then get deathly quiet as if they feared she would eavesdrop on their boisterous conversations.

Fort Laramie always had a surplus of out of work ranch hands. Some were drunks incapable of working more than a day or two at a time and others were content to work only enough to pay for their next beer. Regardless, Caroline needed some men for the roundup.

"I need three men for one or two days to help round up the mustangs. I'll pay three dollars a day plus food. Anybody caught drinking will be sent home without pay. You need to be able to leave with me right now. Raise your hand if you're interested," Caroline bellowed across the room.

Six men raised their hand. Two of the men, Lucky Shoat and Reese Damone, had helped her before and done an adequate job. Caroline selected them and then looked over the other four men. She wasn't familiar with three of the men and the fourth was an old drunk by the name of Scully Wills. Scully had been a top ranch hand in his day and had worked for Caroline's daddy before the bottle had gotten him fired from just about every ranch in the area.

"Scully, can you stay dry for me for a couple of days?" Caroline asked.

Scully nodded his head and managed a sad smile. His expression made Caroline nostalgic over her childhood when the cowboy had worked for her daddy and would bring her licorice back whenever he made a trek into town. He'd always smile at watching her devour the candy as if her joy was one of the best things in the world. The memory made her feel misty and nostalgic. She wished that she knew how to help the old man beat his demon.

"I'm holding you to your word. Let's go," Caroline said and headed for the door.

After returning to the ranch, Caroline led the men into the bunkhouse. Dan, in anticipation of the extra men, had a big pot of hash cooking on the stove.

"After you eat, Bart can show you where to put your horses in the barn and feed them. We will head out at sunrise. Everybody get a good night of sleep," Caroline said before heading to the house.

True to her word, Caroline returned to the bunkhouse just as morning's first gray light appeared. She found Dan standing over the stove frying eggs and bacon. The other men sat at the table waiting for the food to cook. Taking a seat beside Bart, Caroline joined the men for breakfast. She watched as Scully used both of his shaky hands to bring the cup up to his lips and guzzle coffee as an antidote to his usual belt of whiskey. As they ate, she and Dan discussed the plans for the day. The other men listened attentively, but offered no suggestions. Once the meal was eaten, the dishes were deposited into a tub of soapy water and everyone headed to the barn to saddle the horses.

Caroline insisted on riding to see the dead horses. Wolves, coyotes, and buzzards had made a frenzied feast out of the remains. Some of the horses' ribcages were stripped bare of meat and the white bone reflected the rays of the sun. The young ranch owner covered her mouth with her hand in horror at the sight and closed her eyes for a moment to steel herself. Her imagination of what the scene looked like proved no match for the actual carnage.

"It takes a cruel mind to do something like that," Caroline said to no one in particular.

"Yes, it does, Miss Caroline," Dan said to end the awkward silence.

"I remember when that dead stallion down there was still young and didn't even have his own herd yet. He sure was a prideful thing. Enough reminiscing, let's go find some mustangs," Caroline said, turning her horse and riding off the slaughter.

The group rode around a series of foothills until they came to a large meadow that separated the next set of hills. Nearly seventy mustangs grazed on the lush grass. A few of the lead mares raised their heads at the riders and sniffed the air.

"The killing of those other horses must have scared these into grouping up for there to be so many together," Scully surmised.

The others all turned and looked at Scully in surprise that the old man still had lucid thoughts when sober.

"Let's ride back around this last hill and get behind them," Caroline said.

Successfully driving mustangs required basically the same procedure that it did with cattle. A couple of riders would bring up the rear and the others would ride on each side of the herd. The key to moving the horses was to avoid startling the herd and to calmly guide them in the direction of the ranch. Caroline's daddy had built a v-shaped wooden fence with each side running for more than two hundred yards with the mouth being a hundred yards wide. The bottom of the v had a gate to a fenced pasture. Once the mustangs were driven between the two sides of the v, they were then funneled down to the gate and shut in the pasture.

The riders maneuvered into place and slowly approached the mustangs. Some of the older mares had been through the ritual enough times that they began moving without resistance. Stallions became agitated and pranced about and snorted. The younger horses were used to following the lead mares away from danger while the stallions would stay to fight and they started moving with the older mares. A couple of the stallions ran to the rear of the herd and glared at the approaching riders before turning, kicking up their rears, and joining the others.

Driving the horse herd back to the ranch took nearly two hours. As the mustangs entered the v-shaped fence, the riders spread out behind the herd and slowly drove them towards the gate to avoid panicking the horses as the enclosure narrowed. After the first mares walked through the gate entrance, they took off in a run across the pasture and the others followed. Dan loped his horse up to the gate and closed it.

"That's a good start," Dan said as the others joined him.

"Let's get back out there and find some more," Caroline said in her no nonsense manner before turning her horse and riding away at a lope.

Caroline led the group farther north where the foothills grew taller and the mustangs tended to bunch up more with fewer grazing spots. They were riding between two foothills when a barrage of gunfire erupted from the backside of the second rise. The rancher pulled her horse to a hard stop and looked at the others with a stunned look upon her face.

"Do you think they're after the mustangs again?" Caroline asked.

Without bothering to reply, Dan turned his horse and began spurring the animal up the incline of the foothill. The others followed up the steep grade. Near the top of the hill, Dan stopped his horse and pulled his Winchester from the scabbard. After dismounting, he ran to the apex. Four riders were chasing a large herd of mustangs through a long plateau that ran between the mountains. Three horses had already been downed.

"What do you want to do?" Dan asked as the others joined him with guns in hand.

"Everybody shoot in front of the riders and let's hope they stop. I don't want to start a war," Caroline said as she raised her rifle.

Everyone but Scully had a gun and the five of them sent a volley of shots into the ground in front of the riders. The men down below pulled their horses up hard. One animal lost its balance and went down on its front knees before regaining its footing. The four riders sat on their horses looking up towards the higher ground where the shots had been fired.

"If they don't turn around we'll have to shoot their horses out from under them when they get in range. My daddy worked too hard for me to let one of these cattle ranchers ruin us," Caroline said as she chambered another round into her rifle.

One of the men made a big sweeping gesture with his arm and the riders turned their horses and retreated in a gallop.

Caroline let out a sigh so loudly that the others glanced at her.

"Did anybody recognize any of them?" she asked.

"Too far away," Dan replied.

"Do you think by standing up to them that this will be the end of it?" Caroline asked in the hopes of getting some reassurance from one of the men.

Scully walked up beside her. "I'm afeared you just stirred the hornet's nest. Pride usually wins out over common sense and some rancher isn't going to be happy that his men got embarrassed, especially by a woman," he said.

"We better try to find that herd before they run clear to Nebraska," Caroline said.

"Everybody keep their eyes peeled out for those men. I doubt they'll come back, but it never hurts to be aware," Dan said.

Down on the plateau, Dan checked on the three downed mustangs. The sight of two of them still breathing pained the ranch hand. He pulled out his revolver and put them out of their misery with shots to the head that echoed against the surrounding hills.

Caroline and her men found the mustangs about a mile away, standing around resting. They could see that the horses were covered in lather and still breathing hard as they approached. The winded animals provided no resistance as the riders took their places and began coaxing the herd into a walk. Once the mustangs entered the v-shaped fence back at the ranch, Dan raced around on the outside and opened the gate. The tired horses joined the other captured mustangs in the pasture.

"Let's call it day. I've had all the excitement I can stand. We caught a good number of horses today. We can find some more tomorrow," Caroline said as she climbed down from Buddy and started walking the horse towards home. She used her horse to shield her view from the others and rubbed her sore ass. Too much time had passed since she last spent a full day in the saddle.

The second day of rounding up horses went better than the first. They found no dead mustangs and never encountered any other cowboys. By midafternoon, they had captured all the mustangs that the ranch could handle. As Caroline looked out over the horses, she estimated that the roundup could be their biggest ever. She even managed a rare smile when she thanked and congratulated the crew for a job well done.

Caroline paid Lucky, Reese, and Scully their wages. She pulled Scully to the side as the other two men rode for town.

"Scully, why don't you stay here and help for a little while longer. I could use the extra help in sorting out the herd," Caroline said.

The old man looked at her and smiled. "Miss Caroline, you know that I'll only disappoint you if I stay," Scully said.

"You have gone two whole days without a drink. Each day when you get up just tell yourself that you can make it for one more day," she said.

"I'll give it a try. I could use the money," he said.

"That's what I want to hear. I know you can do it," Caroline encouraged.

"Miss Caroline, I know what I am," Scully said sadly.

"And I remember what you were," she said. Her comment made her think about her own changes over the last few years. She remembered the girl that used to like to play pranks on the ranch hands and help her mother bake them cakes on their birthdays. The memory made her realize that neither she nor Scully were any the better for having succumbed to life's difficulties.

Chapter 11

Peace and calm had fallen upon Britt Roberts' home since the death of her husband Charles and had brought a welcome relief to the widow. She felt guilt ridden that she did not miss him or even mourn the man. Every time that she glanced at her arm, still in a splint, she was reminded of the cruelty of her husband. Even before Charles became a drunk, he had proved to be an insensitive man with a volatile temper. When she thought back to their courting days, she could no longer remember what she had ever seen in him. Her family had certainly been right about their misgivings about the union.

Walking to a window, Britt watched her two children playing in the yard. She hoped they were young enough that their father's conduct would fade from their memories and never be an example of acceptable behavior. Only Charles' mother seemed to have any interest in contact with the children. Hazel Roberts had come to see her grandchildren the previous day after church on what proved an awkward visit considering that her family was contesting Charles' will for possession of the home and all the farmland. Britt tried not to worry about the will by taking comfort in the knowledge that she and the children could always live with her parents.

She had gone to town and spoken with her lawyer Thomas Jacobs. The attorney had assured her that the will was airtight as long as the court reached a reasonable decision. The inference that Judge Claiborne might rule in favor of his cronies was not lost on the young woman. No matter the outcome, she was ready to put the will behind her and looked forward to going to court the following day to get the case settled.

∞

Judge Claiborne made Sheriff Briar mighty nervous. The sheriff willingly carried out the judge's nefarious work, but that didn't mean that he enjoyed being in the presence of the old man. After eating his meal at the diner, Sheriff Briar walked to the judge's home and knocked on the door. Through the glass in the door, the sheriff could see the judge lumbering towards the entrance.

"What do you want?" Judge Claiborne asked as a way of a greeting.

"I need to talk to you," Sheriff Briar said.

The judge looked up and down the street to see if anyone were watching. "This better be important," he said before turning and walking towards his office without bothering to invite the sheriff into his home.

Sheriff Briar followed the judge into the home and to the office. Judge Claiborne shut the door before taking a seat at his desk.

"Sit down and tell me what is all so important that the mouse has to come running to the big, bad cat," Judge Claiborne bellowed.

The sheriff sheepishly took a seat. "Last week Albert Roberts and his boys paid me a visit wanting me to talk to Nils again about Caleb. As you can imagine, they weren't too pleasant about it. Anyway, I talked to Nils and didn't learn anything new. I then rode over and told Albert. Well, Albert came back to my office raising a ruckus that they took it upon themselves to go have a talk with Nils and that Olivia came out with a shotgun and ran them off the property. They wanted me to arrest her and I told them that she had a right to make them leave. But here's the interesting thing. Albert let it slip that Olivia told them that Nils sold U.S. Marshal Lucien Eaton a horse last year and that they were friendly with him and would contact him if Albert didn't leave them alone. Now, Judge, I wouldn't think of telling you how to do your job, but if things don't go the way that the Berg family thinks it should, and they get the Feds involved, we all could have trouble on our hands," he said.

The judge removed the top from a glass decanter sitting on his desk and poured himself a glass of brandy without offering the sheriff any of the liquor. He leaned back in his chair and took a sip, savoring the taste as he contemplated the sheriff's news. "This is very good information. I trust that you haven't told anyone else," the judge said.

"Not a soul," Sheriff Briar replied.

"Good. Keep it that way," Judge Claiborne said before pulling two cigars from his humidor and handing one to the sheriff. "Have a good evening."

∞

On the day of the hearing, Nils, Olivia, and the two children sat on the front row and Britt sat with her lawyer Thomas Jacobs as Judge Claiborne called the court into session. The Roberts had retained the judge's former law partner Innis Wicker as their attorney. Wicker was another one of the men knee deep in the shenanigans that went on in Chalksville and had business interest with the judge and the Roberts family. Sheriff Briar sat in the back of the room, anxious to see how the judge would rule.

Albert and Michael Roberts were called to the stand and testified that Charles had complained to them that Britt had forced the terms of the will upon her husband in exchange for preserving their marriage. Thomas Jacobs tried to call their statements into question, but had little recourse to prove otherwise with the nature of the hearsay testimony.

Britt next took the stand and watched warily as Innis Wicker approached her.

"Mrs. Roberts, isn't it true that after an altercation with your husband you forced Charles Roberts to agree to the terms of this will if he wanted to save the marriage?" Innis asked.

"No, it is not. I insisted on a will, but we both agreed to the terms based on what would be best for our children," Britt answered.

"Mrs. Roberts, may I remind you that you are under oath," the lawyer said.

"You mean just like Albert and Michael were supposed to be?" Britt asked.

Judge Claiborne rapped his gavel. "Mrs. Roberts will kindly answer the questions that are asked. Mr. Wicker, I would remind you that Mrs. Roberts was just sworn in and understands her duties. Do not waste the courts time with fallacious commentary," he said.

The lawyer gave the judge a contentious look before turning his attention back to Britt.

"Is it true that you had your brother kill your husband in order to receive all of Charles's property?" Innis asked.

"No, I did not," Britt said with indignation.

"Nothing further," Innis said before taking his seat.

Thomas Jacobs arose from his seat and questioned Britt. He allowed her the opportunity to explain all that had gone into the decision making for drafting the will.

After Britt finished expounding her testimony, he took his seat.

Anxious to bring the proceedings to a close, Judge Claiborne looked at Britt and then over at the Roberts family. He tried to steel his nerves as he prepared to make his ruling. Innis and the Roberts would all be incensed. "In the interest of determining the owner of the contested land with spring planting shortly upon us, I have chosen to expedite my decision in this case. I read the will this morning. Upon reading the document and listening to the testimony here today, I find no grounds to contest this will and rule in favor of the defendant. Furthermore, I am for the record warning the Roberts family to leave Britt Roberts and the Berg family alone. I see Sheriff Briar sitting in this court and I am trusting him to make sure that my orders are obeyed. Until Charles Roberts' killer is brought to trial, I do not expect to see any of the parties involved in this hearing in my court," he said before rapping his gavel and walking out of the chamber.

Britt embraced her lawyer before walking to her family and giving each of them a hug while Albert and Michael glared in their direction. The family practically skipped out of the courthouse and headed for home.

Albert turned towards his family. "You all stay here," he said before walking past the witness stand and through the door that led to the offices. Opening the door to Judge Claiborne's office, he barged in and slammed the door.

"What are you doing in here?" Judge Claiborne asked irritably.

"You know damn well what I'm doing here. What in the hell was that all about?" Albert asked.

"A little bird told me that the Bergs know U.S. Marshal Eaton. You and I have a lot bigger fish to fry than Charles' house and one hundred and sixty acres. If the Feds ever started nosing around here, you and I could both end up in prison for some of the things we've pulled. Now you had better leave the Bergs alone or you'll be dealing with me. I will not go to prison over your greed and revenge. I'm sorry for the loss of Charles, but those people didn't have a damn thing to do with it. And if the damn fool would have kept his nose out of the bottle and treated Britt like the fine woman that she is, he wouldn't be dead now. If I were her brother, I would have killed his sorry ass too. Now get out of my office," the judge yelled.

Albert looked at the Judge Claiborne as if he were seeing him for the first time. He could barely control his anger and had to suppress the urge to punch the judge, but at the same time, he feared the man. The judge looked scared and desperate to keep the U.S. Marshal out of Chalksville. Albert had learned a long time ago that nothing on earth proved to be as dangerous as a desperate man. "I'll be no more trouble," he said meekly before walking out of the office.

Chapter 12

Caleb and Joey rode into Fort Laramie twelve days after their encounter with the boy on the stolen horse. The rest of the trip had been uneventful except for a day of heavy rains that had made travel and sleeping miserable. Along the way, they had stopped at Fort Kearny, finding the place in flux as soldiers bustled about preparing to close the once vital post in a mere matter of days. As they had traveled farther west, Caleb would gaze at the horizon in awe of the vastness of the land and the lack of trees. For a Tennessean that had never before been west of the Mississippi, the change in terrain seemed almost incomprehensible and he would babble to Joey about it for miles. When they reached Courthouse and Jail Rock, Caleb had been so stunned at the rock formations that he had insisted, much to Joey's chagrin, that they travel several miles out of their way to get a closer look. At Chimney Rock, Caleb had climbed halfway up the base before looking back and grinning like a child. Joey, watching from his horse, realized that for the first time he was catching a glimpse of what the young man must have been like before the deaths of his wife and child. From his high vantage point, Caleb could see for miles and decided on the spot that he loved the west.

"If I were a smart man I'd stop to have a couple of beers before we ride to the ranch. It might make all the hell I'm going to catch from Caroline a tad more bearable," Joey said as they rode past the Fort Laramie Saloon.

"Why do you stay with her if she is that bad?" Caleb asked.

"I promised her daddy that if anything ever happened to him that I would look out for Caroline and Claire. I'm a man of my word. And besides, her bark is a lot worse than her bite," Joey answered.

"Maybe I should just get a room here and find me a job elsewhere," Caleb said.

"I won't hear of it. Whether you come to work for us or not, you can stay over in the bunkhouse. I owe you that. And you're a horseman by trade. Putting up with Caroline is preferable to working with dumb old cattle," Joey said.

Grinning, Caleb said, "I don't know. Sounds like I'd deal with a lot of bull either way."

"Come on. Let's get to the ranch. I'm ready to get this butt out of a saddle," Joey said as he nudged his horse into a trot.

On the ride to the ranch, Caleb continued to talk with astonishment of the rugged landscape and his love of its beauty. Joey warned the young man that he might have a different view come wintertime. They arrived at the ranch just before noon and could see Caroline and the ranch hands working in the pasture. Joey showed Caleb to the barn where they put the horses up and fed them before walking to the bunkhouse.

"They'll be coming in for lunch here in a minute. I'll leave you with the boys while I go talk to Caroline. She usually takes her meal with her mother. I'll introduce you to her when the time is right," Joey said as he began making a pot of coffee.

As the ranch hands entered the bunkhouse for lunch, Joey introduced Caleb to Dan, Bart, and Scully.

"I hope you brought Caroline a box of chocolates. She's been ranting about you every day that we're out there working," Dan said.

"I might as well go and get this over with," Joey said and walked out of the bunkhouse.

Claire answered the knock on the door from Joey.

"Joey, welcome home. How is your mother?" Claire asked.

"Thank you, ma'am. She's still going strong and feisty as ever," Joey answered.

"Caroline is waiting for you in the office. She saw you ride in," Claire said and gave the ranch hand a sympathetic wink.

"Thank you, Mrs. Langley," Joey said as he removed his hat.

"Joey, I've told you a hundred times to call me Claire. We've known each other way too long for such formality," she said.

"If this doesn't prove to be our last meeting, I'll do better," Joey said.

Leaning in close, Claire quietly said, "Stand up for yourself. That girl can get a little too big for her britches every now and then. Her daddy would have straightened her out a long time ago."

Smiling, Joey walked back to the office, finding Caroline sitting at her desk. He took a seat across from her and waited for her to speak first. Caroline glared at Joey and seemed to be in a battle of wills as to which one of them would speak first.

"You completely missed out on the roundup and the separating of the herd. Some of the mares have already begun to foal. We will be turning out the stallions in a day or two. And to top it off, one of our neighbors had started killing the mustangs before we rounded them up. When I agreed to let you go back east, I thought you would have enough respect for the ranch to get back here on time. I guess I was wrong about that," Caroline said in an icy tone.

"Caroline, I would have been here right on time if a spring snow hadn't buried everything back home. The roads were drifted shut for two weeks," Joey said.

"Joey, I don't want to hear it. If you had taken the train as I suggested, this would have never happened. This isn't the good old days. And I haven't even mentioned the fact that you got robbed and I had to advance you money," she said.

"I know that. I just wanted ..." he said.

"I don't care what you wanted. I don't even know why I need you around here. It would seem the ranch runs just fine without you. And Scully is working out well. He has gone two weeks without a drink," Caroline said, staring Joey in the eye.

"Can I talk now?" Joey said in an exasperated tone that he had never before taken with the young woman. He could see the surprise on Caroline's face and knew that she was taken aback by his question.

Caroline nodded her head.

"First off, I am truly sorry about my delay in getting back here and I do appreciate you letting me go. And you are right in that I should have taken the train. I just wanted to make that ride one more time before I get too old. You'll understand someday. I do have most of your precious money and an extra horse that I can sell to pay you the rest. It seems your money is more of a concern to you than the fact that I could have been killed. If you want to fire me, you have that right. Go ahead and get it over with, but either way, I've heard all the sassing that I'm going to listen to from you. Just let me know whether I'm needed around here or not," Joey said and stood. With Caroline's bad temper, he expected to see her skin turn from pink to beet red, but instead found the color draining from the young woman's face as she leaned back in her chair.

"Joey, please sit back down," Caroline said in a conciliatory voice and waited until the ranch hand had taken his seat. "I'm sorry I gave the impression that the money is more important than your well-being. That certainly is not the case. You have been way too much a part of my life for me ever to feel that way. And while I admit that I'm still irritated by this whole affair, I should have taken a more measured tone. We both know that I need you here. Please forgive my outburst."

"Apology accepted. Let's just move on," Joey said.

"Thank you," she said.

"Caroline, unless word of my return puts a stop to things, we're going to have a fight to keep this place going. Somebody wants you out of the way," Joey said.

"I know. I've been staying up at night worrying about the horses we turned back out. I rode out and had a talk with Loren, Thomas, and Nathan. Of course, none of them admitted to having anything to do with the horse killings," Caroline said.

"I wouldn't expect otherwise," Joey said.

"I think at least one of them has to be behind it," she said.

"The fellow that helped me out after I got robbed is in the bunkhouse. His name is Caleb Gunnar. I would've been in a fix if not for him and he's as loyal as the day is long. We caught up with the robbers and killed them. He could have just ridden on, but he stayed. He certainly didn't have a dog in the hunt. He's good with a gun and knows horses as well as anybody I've ever met. And on top of that, he rides a stallion that is the finest horse I've ever laid eyes on. I'd like you to meet him and see what you think. I think he could be real handy to have around here, especially if we have trouble. That stallion sure would be good for our breeding program too," Joey said.

"I wondered who rode in with you, but Joey, I don't know if we need another hand. Scully is like his old self. That's a lot of salary I'd be paying," Caroline said.

"I think the world of Scully, but he will eventually let you down. He's climbed back into the bottle too many times to ever change now. Just meet Caleb and decide then. That's all I'm asking. I'm telling you that the man knows horseflesh and I do owe him for all he's done for me," Joey said.

"Very well. Send him on up here, but I'm not making any promises," Caroline said.

"That's all I ask," Joey said before walking out of the office.

Claire met Joey at the door just before the ranch hand walked outside.

"Did you put my daughter in her place?" Claire asked.

"Well, I didn't have to turn her over my knee - yet. We got things worked out," Joey said.

"Good. I thought you would," Claire said.

"Now if I can just get her to hire Caleb," Joey said.

A puzzled look came upon Claire's face.

"I'll tell you about him later," Joey said.

"Please do. Come by tonight after supper and have coffee with me. I'd love to hear about your trip," Claire said.

Joey gave a nod of his head before exiting the house. He walked straight to the bunkhouse to find Caleb and the others chowing down on lunch.

"When you finish, go see Caroline," Joey said to Caleb.

Bart looked up with a grin. With his mouth still full of food, he asked, "Did the boss upbraid you good?"

"Everything is fine. We came to an understanding. You should be more worried what I think about your work," Joey said, effectively ending the conversation.

Caleb took a final drink of water and walked to a shaving mirror mounted on the wall. He used his fingers to rake his hair into some semblance of neatness before walking out of the bunkhouse.

Claire, curious to meet the new mystery man, greeted Caleb at the door. The sight of the tall young man caught her by surprise and she had to clench her lips together tightly to keep from grinning like a Cheshire cat. She wanted to giggle at the thought of her persnickety daughter meeting the good-looking Caleb.

"You must be Caleb," Claire said.

"Yes, ma'am. Nice to meet you," Caleb said.

"I believe I hear a southern accent. Call me Claire," she said.

"I'm from Tennessee, ma ... Claire," he said.

"Good to meet you. I'm Caroline's mother. I'll show you to her office," Claire said and started walking.

Caroline stood and held out her hand to shake as Caleb walked into the office. As Caleb shook with Caroline, he tried to take in all of her features. In his mind's eye, Caroline had been taller than he was and looked like some ogre. The sight of the petite young woman caught him totally off guard. She was right pretty even with her brown hair pinned so tightly to her head that she looked like a boy. Her brown eyes had a fire to them that let you know she was somebody to be reckoned with. The men's clothing that she wore did nothing to flatter her figure, but the suspenders running to the side of her breasts made the mounds stand out prominently and he had to force himself not to stare.

"I'm Caleb Gunnar," he said.

"I'm Caroline Langley. Please have a seat," she said.

Touching Caleb's hand had sent a jolt into an area of Caroline's body that hadn't had a jolt in a long time and the feeling made her take an instant dislike towards him. She already regretted letting Joey talk her into meeting his new friend. To her way of thinking, he looked to be a pretty boy used to having his way with woman and she certainly would have none of that.

"You have a nice place here, ma'am," Caleb said to break the silence.

"Thank you. Joey says you know horses. What's your story?" Caroline asked in her no-nonsense manner.

"My daddy had success crossing Arabian and Quarter horses. He developed a line with both endurance and speed. I've been helping him since I could walk. I guess I've seen just about everything when it comes to horses. I also spent time as a soldier in the war. So I know how to fight if necessary," Caleb said.

The notion that a grown man called his father by the title of daddy struck her as juvenile and Caleb's slow southern speech grated on her nerves. "What made you decide to move out west?" she asked.

Caleb had no desire to tell her any more than necessary about his life but he feared that if he were too vague that she would ask if he were running from the law and he didn't like to lie. "My wife and baby died during delivery. I needed to leave to move on with my life," he said.

Taken aback by the news, Caroline regretted that she had ever asked. Sympathy was the last thing she wanted to feel for Caleb. Wishing to move on from the subject, she said, "I'm sorry for your loss. Losing loved ones is never easy."

"Thank you."

"Joey seems to think a lot of you," Caroline said.

"Ah, Joey is a good fellow. You're lucky to have him. I just helped him out a little. Nothing that anybody else wouldn't have done," Caleb said.

With her sympathy already fading, Caleb's modesty struck a raw nerve. "Joey said that you backed him in a gunfight. I don't consider that a little thing and I don't know why you would either. Caleb, I'm just not sure we have a spot for another ranch hand right now."

"Okay, ma'am. That's fine. I kind of figured you had enough men already. I'm sorry if Joey put you in an uncomfortable spot," Caleb said and stood.

"Why would I be in an uncomfortable spot? I certainly do not owe you anything. Joey is a grown man that should be able to look out for himself," she said haughtily.

Caleb eyed Caroline and made a small grimace. "Everybody needs a little help every now and then. If you think otherwise, I feel sorry for you," he said.

Caroline's eyes lit up like little embers as she peered straight at Caleb. "I will not tolerate sympathy from the likes of you, but I'll give it. If you are such a horseman, I have the horse for you. If you can break Diablo, you can have a job," she spit out.

"No thank you, ma'am. I don't think I can be happy working for you," Caleb said and turned towards the door.

"Just as I expected. Every southerner I've ever met is all talk. I think everyone of you talks so slow just so you can drag out all your ramblings," Caroline said.

Turning back towards her, Caleb tried not to show emotion. Insulting his southern heritage had stung and he didn't want her to know it. "I assume that since Joey is your foreman that he gets paid more than your other ranch hands. If I ride that horse, I want ten dollars a month more than your ranch hands as long as it isn't more than what Joey makes," he said, squaring his shoulders and standing tall.

With a sardonic smile, Caroline eyed her nemesis. She realized that Caleb had painted her into a corner from which she could not escape. "Fine," she said with derision. "If you can ride that horse you will be worth the extra money anyways."

All of the ranch crew were milling around in front of the bunkhouse waiting for Caroline. Joey watched as Caroline and Caleb walked out of the house towards the group. Both of them were walking with too much determination and speed in their steps for the stroll to be casual. The foreman had a bad feeling about things and a resignation that Caleb wouldn't be coming to work for the ranch.

"Dan and Bart, go saddle up Diablo. Mr. Gunnar here is supposed to be a fine horseman and has agreed to show us how to break a horse," Caroline called out before she and Caleb had even reached the group.

Caleb followed Dan and Bart to get a look at the horse he would to attempt to ride.

"Caroline, what do you think you are doing? You're liable to get Caleb killed," Joey said as she approached.

"You are the one that bragged on what a fine horseman Caleb is. I thought we'd find out if it were true. Even I tried to ride Diablo a few weeks ago and I'm just a girl," Caroline said with a touch of sarcasm.

"I never said a thing about Caleb being a bronco buster. I think it's a sapheaded notion for anybody to get on that horse. I told you last fall that the animal is plain loco and we should just shoot it," Joey said.

"You are not much fun today," Caroline said.

"I take it that you didn't hit it off with Caleb," Joey said.

"I did not. I can't say I like your new friend," she said.

Scully stood nearby and realized he had no desire to be privy to their conversation. He walked off towards the corral.

"And why not?" Joey asked.

"What's there to like? I bet his mind works as slow as he talks. There's just something about him that irritates me," Caroline said as she challenged Joey by staring him in the eye.

Joey let out a sigh and tipped his hat back off his forehead. "Caroline, if your daddy were still alive, he'd be ashamed of you. He never treated a person with disrespect and he wouldn't have tolerated it from you by a long shot. One of these days you need to stop being mad at the world just because you made a mistake in marriage. Not every young man is like your ex-husband," he said.

"Don't you dare ..." Caroline said, but Joey walked away from her before she could finish. She watched him as he climbed the corral fence and took a seat on the top board.

Dan and Bart walked the horse into the corral and Caleb followed. The two men got into position to hold the animal while Caleb mounted.

"Tie him to the center post and go take a seat," Caleb said.

"You'll never be able to climb on this crazy thing by yourself," Dan warned.

"I know what I'm doing. Go on, please," Caleb said and waited until the two men took seats beside Joey.

Diablo pulled on the lead rope with all his might and his eyes bulged wildly. Caleb could see that the animal was scared to near hysteria of humans. Somebody had traumatized the horse in the past. Caleb remembered that his daddy always said that a horse could feel your emotions better than you could. He closed his eyes and exhaled slowly, releasing all the tension that Caroline had caused him. Taking hold of the rope, he walked to the horse, putting his hand on the animal's muzzle and willing it his calmness. Diablo continued to pull against the rope but not as forcefully. His eyes, while still showing fear, no longer looked deranged. Caleb stood in that pose talking soothingly to the animal for a good five minutes.

Bart giggled and looked at Dan. "Maybe he plans to talk Diablo into submission," he said.

Caroline had joined the men, standing on the bottom rail so that she could see over the top board. She looked over at Bart. "Shut up and watch. You might learn something for a change," she said.

While slowly moving his free hand, Caleb touched the horse's neck. Diablo pulled harder on the rope for a moment and then relaxed. Caleb again spent minutes talking to the animal before moving back to the saddle. He draped his arms over it and stood a moment. The animal began sidestepping, trying to flee. Caleb returned to the horse's head and talked some more. He repeated going to the saddle five times before Diablo accepted his arms across the saddle and stood still. After standing there a couple of minutes, Caleb put his foot in the stirrup and put some weight into it. Once again, the animal started sidestepping and Caleb repeated the whole process of moving between the animal's head and the saddle until he at last put all his weight into the stirrup and Diablo stood still.

Bart could no longer contain himself. "Maybe he plans to wait until old age sets in the horse," he said.

"Go clean the manure out of all the stalls. I don't want to see you again until you are finished," Caroline said as she glared at her ranch hand. With a hangdog expression on his face, Bart climbed off the fence and walked towards the barn.

Caleb untied the rope from the post, and in a motion so smooth that the horse never had time to move, he climbed aboard Diablo. The horse took off in a dead run around the corral, hopping occasionally but never bucking. Caleb let the animal run until it had worked itself into a lather and began to slow. He then used the rope reins to turn the horse's head and let it run the opposite direction around the corral. Finally, Diablo slowed to a walk and Caleb let the horse make two more circles around the corral before stopping it in front of the bystanders.

"When I finish training Diablo, I want him to be my everyday horse," Caleb said to Caroline.

As much as she had longed to see Caleb fly through the air and fail, Caroline begrudgingly admired his skills with horses. She attempted to stymie a smile, but failed. "You are one fine horseman. Pick any animal you desire," she said.

Chapter 13

The day after Caroline hired Caleb, she asked him to show her Leif. Not wishing to incite the temperamental woman, Caleb stymied a smile before going to retrieve the horse. He proudly led the animal out of the barn on a halter and stopped in front of Caroline.

"Is he ornery?" she asked.

"Not at all. He's as gentle as any gelding you've ever ridden. The only time he's a handful is around mares in season, but even then, he's not mean. Leif is a lover not a fighter," he said with a grin.

Caroline walked around the horse. She begrudgingly had to admit that Joey was right in that the stallion looked better than any stud on the ranch. Leif certainly seemed balanced with good front and rear angles. He appeared well muscled and to be in top condition even after his long journey. His topline was shorter than his underline with good girth and his neck tied into his body properly. As she walked around the horse one more time, she couldn't find a weakness to be able to dismiss the horse's structure.

"Does he move as well as he looks?" Caroline asked.

"He does and at all gaits to boot. Even his trot is smooth," Caleb replied.

"Would you be interested in letting me use him on some of the mares?" she inquired.

"I wouldn't at a salary of forty dollars a month," he replied.

The comment made Caroline grin. "I suppose not. What would it cost?" she asked.

"How much do you get to sell your horses to the army?" Caleb countered.

"I don't see where that is any of your concern," Caroline said brusquely.

"It is if you want me to come up with a price," Caleb said, grinning impishly.

Looking down at her feet, Caroline used the toe of her boot to scratch a mark across the dirt as if she were subconsciously drawing a line in the sand. She didn't appreciate the way that Caleb had a knack for cornering her to get what he wanted. "Between a hundred sixty-five and two hundred dollars," she said reluctantly.

"How about twenty percent of the sale price?" Caleb.

"If you want a percent, why did you need to know the price?" Caroline asked.

"So I'd know how much money to expect from that percent," he said.

"I'll give you fifteen percent of every gelding your horse sires that the army buys, payable upon sale," she said.

"What if I'm not still around by then?" he asked.

"You may not like me, but I'm honest. I'll get your money to you," Caroline said defensively.

"What about the fillies he sires that you breed later?" Caleb questioned. He had to admit to himself that he enjoyed sparing with Caroline as long as she remained civil. The woman certainly had a good head on her shoulders and a fine business sense.

"I think you are a better horse trader than you are a horseman. I'll give you a onetime payment of forty dollars for any fillies we decide to breed. I'll have to hire an accountant to keep track of all this," she said.

"I get to pick the mares to breed to Leif," Caleb stated.

"No, this is not your ranch. I'll do that with help from Joey," Caroline stated matter-of-factly.

Smiling, Caleb said, "Not if you want to use Leif."

"Mr. Gunnar, I believe that you are an obstinate man. I'm not sure if it's because I'm a woman or it's just your nature. Whatever the reason, I find it tiring," she said.

Hearing someone speak his new surname for the first time gave Caleb a melancholy moment and made him long for his family back home. When he refocused his attention on the problem at hand, Caleb said, "I wouldn't say that it's my true nature and it has nothing to do with the fact that you're a woman. It has everything to do with the fact that you are ill tempered and pushy. However, to prove that I can be reasonable, I suggest we practice the art of compromise. We both must mutually agree to the suitable mares for Leif," he said.

Caroline scowled at Caleb to hide her hurt. His assessment of her had stung even if she knew that if she were being honest with herself that she would have to agree with him. She also had to admit that she admired his honesty though she would never tell him so. "You know that there is no law keeping you here. You are free to go," she said.

"You challenged my southern heritage and it came back to bite you in a most unfortunate spot. So, no, I'm staying. You'll have to deal with it. Now do we have a deal on Leif or not?' Caleb asked.

"We do," Caroline said before turning and marching towards the house.

"For the record, I do admire your tenacity in running this ranch, just not how you go about it," Caleb called out to her.

Walking into the house, Caroline slammed the front door and marched to her office. Claire came hurrying after her.

"Is something wrong?" Claire asked.

"Caleb Gunnar is the most hardheaded man I have ever seen in my life. I'd like to knock his block off," Caroline vented.

"In other words, you can't push him around," Claire said.

"Mother, on whose side are you?" Caroline asked.

"Why did you hire him then?" her mother asked, avoiding answering the question.

"Because I shot my big mouth off and he painted me into a corner with it. Don't let that slow southern accent fool you. He is too smart for his own good," Caroline said.

"Too smart for your own good, you mean," Claire corrected.

Glaring at her mother, Caroline said, "You might think this is all amusing now, but you won't like him once you get to know him."

Claire turned and walked away towards the front of the house smiling at the thought that she already did like Caleb Gunnar. Glancing out the front window, she saw Joey approaching Caleb who still stood in front of the barn brushing down his stallion. The sight of Joey made Claire smile. Her after-dinner coffee with him the night before had been an enjoyable time. She missed the camaraderie of a man since the death of her husband. Every opportunity that she could finesse into spending time with the ranch foreman, she made sure to take. Joey certainly knew how to be entertaining and he had her in stitches with his talk of walking down the trail in his long underwear. In the back of her mind, she still had hopes of encouraging him to court her.

Joey walked up to Leif and patted the horse on the neck. "What did you say to Caroline to get her all worked up? She looked like a wet hen stomping towards the house," he said.

"We were negotiating the use of Leif on some mares and I told her what I thought of her. She didn't much care for it," Caleb said with a grin.

"Oh, my. I can see that you're determined to be a burr under her saddle. Give her a little slack. She's been through a lot," Joey said.

"So have I and I don't go around mad at the world. She needs to mind her manners," Caleb said.

"No, but you prefer to keep your own company and shut yourself off from people now," Joey said as he looked Caleb in the eye.

"You don't know that I was ever any different. You didn't know me before," Caleb said with irritation.

"I've spent enough time with you these last few weeks to know who you are and to get glimpses of what you once were. Every once in a while you let that guard down and I can see someone that used to be carefree and loved life. If I'm wrong, look me in the eye and tell me so. I'll apologize and never mention it again," Joey said, never wavering in his stare.

Caleb averted his eyes and concentrated on brushing his horse a moment before looking back at Joey and giving a melancholy smile. "You're probably right. I don't mean to be. It's just who I am now. If I offended you on the trail, I'm sorry," Caleb said.

"You were fine and even good company most the time. I don't know what I would have done without you. I just want you to realize that life has changed both you and Caroline in different ways and not for the better. Just something to think about," Joey said.

Grinning, Caleb said, "My momma would call you a sage. She's a teacher and likes to use words like that. I'll keep what you said in mind."

"Tonight I'm headed for town to the saloon. I thought it might put a stop to the troubles if people see that I'm back around the ranch. I'll buy you a beer if you want to come with me," Joey said.

"I think I'll pass. I've done all the riding I want to do for a while. Never was much for saloons anyways. Maybe next time," Caleb said.

"Suit yourself," Joey said before heading to the bunkhouse.

After eating supper with the rest of the crew, Joey helped feed and brush down the horses in the barn before mounting up and heading towards town. He rode at a leisurely pace, enjoying the solitude. All the time on the trail with Caleb and now the confines of the bunkhouse had left him appreciative of his own occasional company. Staring off at the mountains, he marveled at their majesty again as if seeing them for the first time. He arrived in town and tied his horse in front of the mercantile. Rushing into the store just before it closed for the night, he bought some cigars before walking to the Fort Laramie Saloon.

Inside the crowded saloon, Joey looked around to see ranch hands from all three of neighboring ranches. He walked up to the bar and ordered a beer. Ned, the bartender, greeted him like an old lost friend and a steady stream of cowboys came up to greet him and welcome him back. He wasn't surprised that the cowboys from the Sanders ranch sat together at a table and never greeted him. Loren liked to hire ranch hands like himself that never tended to be very social. Joey did find it odd that nobody from either the Rhodes or Horn spreads had spoken to him. The men had pulled two tables together and were sitting around laughing and carrying on amongst themselves. In the past, he had always gotten along well with both crews and even gone hunting with a couple of the men. Ordering a second beer, Joey walked over to the tables and grabbed an empty chair.

"How have all you boys been?" Joey asked as he took a seat.

"Well if it isn't long lost Joey Clemson. We all figured that you finally got tired of taking marching orders from that she-devil and hightailed it to greener pastures," Frankie Myers said.

Frankie prided himself in being the wiseacre amongst the cowboys and his big mouth had gotten him laid out flat on more than one occasion. He had worked for Nathan Horn for years. Joey usually just ignored Frankie - a snappy comeback would go to waste as it sailed over the cowboy's head.

"Nah, I just visited my mom this winter. I like working for Caroline. She's a sight easier on the eyes than your boss," Joey replied.

The other cowboys chuckled and Frankie looked embarrassed. He looked down at the table before taking a drink of beer.

"Say what you want, but I sure wouldn't take orders from no woman," Frankie counted.

Not wishing to engage the ranch hand further, Joey ignored the comment. "Any of you boys hear anything about somebody killing mustangs on the open range?" he asked.

An awkward silence followed before Frankie said, "Are you accusing us?"

"I'm not accusing anybody. I'm just trying to find out if anybody has heard anything," Joey said.

"Killing off those damn mustangs would be the best thing that could happen. This is cattle country and those horses are hell on the grass," Frankie said.

"Our ranch depends on those animals for our livelihood and they have as much right to graze on the open range as your cattle. If anybody tries to kill off those herds, well, then they're asking for a war," Joey said as he stared down Frankie.

"None of us know anything about it. Let's change the subject," Frankie said.

Joey nodded his head. Pulling out his new revolver, he showed off the gun that he bought on the trail with Caleb. He stayed at the table talking with the cowboys until he finished his beer. Deciding that it wasn't worth his time to try to talk to the Sanders crew, he moved to a table of card players and joined the game. For the next couple of hours, Joey passed the time playing cards and drinking beer until he determined he needed to head home. He said his goodbyes and walked out the door.

As Joey walked down the boardwalk towards his horse, he pulled one of his newly purchased cigars from his jacket and gave it a lick. As he reached into his pocket for a match, he suddenly spiraled to the ground from a blow to the skull from something hard. Before he had time even to grab his head, he felt himself being dragged into the alley. A kick to the stomach knocked the air out of his lungs and another blow smashed into his ribs. Joey couldn't see his attackers in the dark alley but sensed there were more than one. As he tried to breathe, somebody flipped him onto his back and sat on him as they pounded his face with their fists.

"That's enough. Don't kill him," a voice called out.

"Tell your bunch that the next time they shoot in our direction they better kill us," another voice growled before delivering one final blow. The assailants ran off into the darkness.

Joey curled up in a fetal position, trying to get air back into his lungs and clear his head. His mind seemed to be working as if in a haze as he worked to comprehend what had just happened. He tried to recall the sound of the men's voices but could barely even remember what had been said. The fogginess seemed to grow worse, and despite his best effort, he drifted off into unconsciousness. When he awoke, he had no idea how long he had been out, but the sky still looked dark. He managed to get to his feet and stumble to his horse. Each breath produced a sharp pain in his side and his head felt as if a blacksmith's hammer was trying to flatten his skull. Pulling himself into the saddle with a groan of pain, he headed for home unable to allow his horse to go any faster than a walk. The ride seemed to last forever and by the time he reached the ranch, he could see the sky to the east just beginning to change from black to gray.

As he stumbled into the bunkhouse, Joey hollered, "Boys, somebody beat the snot out of me and I sure could use some help."

Always a light sleeper, Caleb jumped up and found the oil lamp before the others had stirred. He struck a match and lit the wick. As he placed the globe in place, Caleb saw Joey standing in the doorway using the frame for a support. Joey's face looked a mess. One eye was blackened and swelling shut. He had a knot on his cheekbone that looked as if the skin could burst and his lips were busted and puffy. Caleb rushed to his friend and helped him to a chair at the table.

"What happened?" Caleb asked.

Joey pondered the question a moment as he tried to think. "I believe I got waylaid walking to my horse to come home. My minds not working so good," he said.

Dan walked up from behind Joey and said, "He's got a goose egg on the back of his head."

Caleb reached around and touched the back of Joey's head. "Oh, my. No wonder you can't think straight. I'd bet you have a concussion. Are you hurt anywhere else?" he asked.

"It hurts to breathe. I think I got some cracked ribs," Joey answered.

"What do you want me to do?" Dan asked.

"You better go get Caroline and Claire. I'm not much of a doctor," Caleb replied.

"No, don't go making a fuss. I've been hurt worse falling off a horse," Joey said.

Looking up at Dan, Caleb made a single nod of his head towards the door and the ranch hand slipped outside. Caleb retrieved a pan of water and used a rag to start cleaning away the dried blood on Joey's face. He didn't know what else to do and decided it best to wait for the women.

"Do you have any idea why they beat you?" Caleb asked.

Joey looked up blankly at Caleb and winced as he attempted to rub the knot on the back of his head. "It's over the mustangs. Somebody told me that the next time one of us shot at them that we had better aim to kill. I'd warned some of them earlier that things needed to stop," he said.

"Did you see any of them?" Caleb further inquired.

"Not a soul. I don't feel much like talking," Joey replied.

Caroline and Claire, along with Dan, came barreling into the bunkhouse as if they were racing. The two women still wore their nightgowns covered in housecoats. Claire carried a bag of medical supplies that she had used through the years to treat the various injuries common to ranch work. As the ranch's default doctor, she had gotten good at treating cuts, bites, and just about anything else thrown her way.

"Dan told me that Joey hurts when he breathes. Get his shirt off and let me check his ribs," Claire ordered.

Caroline stepped in front of Caleb and began unbuttoning Joey's shirt. Her eyes welled with tears as she gently worked.

"I must be a sight to make you cry," Joey said.

Looking embarrassed, Caroline said, "Oh, hush. I was just thinking about how I'll have to start doing all your work again."

Claire pressed on the bruised spot on Joey's rib. He winced and let out a groan.

"Careful there. If you break it, you buy it," Joey said, attempting humor.

"I'm pretty sure those ribs are cracked," Claire said as she retrieved a roll of gauze and began wrapping them around Joey's torso.

"I'll be good as new in a few days," Joey said.

After finishing the bandaging, Claire examined Joey's head and face. "Not much I can do about the rest of it. Caleb and Dan, would you be so kind as to help Joey to the house. We'll put him in the spare bedroom," she said.

"Hold it a minute. I'll not be a burden. I'm going to crawl into my bunk," Joey protested.

"I will not hear of it. Everybody else will be working in just a little while. You'll need tending to for a couple of days. You could start coughing up blood or lose consciousness. Caroline is not the only one that knows how to be bossy," Claire said and smiled at her daughter. "Now let's go."

Chapter 14

Just before noon, Joey awoke in the spare bedroom of the Langley home. He looked around the unfamiliar room as he tried to get his wits about him. As he turned his head to the right, he saw Claire sitting in a chair near the wall busily crocheting a doily.

Feeling his eyes upon her, Claire looked up and smiled. "How are you feeling?" she asked.

"Like I lost a battle with a train," Joey replied.

"You look like it too," she said as she gazed at his face. His left eye was completely swollen shut and his lips were puffed up to twice their normal size.

Joey chuckled and then winced in pain. "I never had much to work with in the first place," he said.

"Oh, you are being modest now. Seriously, how do you feel?" Claire asked.

"My head's pounding and it hurts to breathe. I've had cracked ribs before and I'd say I have them again. My mind is working better than last night that's for sure. Not that I can remember anything new about what happened, but I'm not all foggy," Joey said.

"You just need some rest for a while and you'll be good as new. I'll take plenty good care of you," she said.

"I never meant to be such a burden. Between getting back from Illinois late, and now this, Caroline is going to ship me out. How can I ever repay you?" he asked.

"Don't you worry about Caroline. She knows you butter her bread, and besides, I'm still her mother and will always have the last word," Claire said with a smile before pausing a moment to embolden herself. "I'll tell you how you can repay me. I have a fine buggy that only gets used to go to church. It sure would be nice to have a man take me to town for a nice meal and a ride out into the country."

Joey peered over at Claire and could see her blushing. Her proposal caught him so off guard that he felt tongue-tied. His mind raced with thoughts of the fit that Caroline would undoubtedly throw and the potential awkwardness that could follow. But on the other hand, Claire was a fine looking woman and as sweet as they come. He wasn't about to pass on an opportunity to spend time with her. "Uh, Claire, I would consider taking you out an honor. As soon as I am better, we'll make a date of it," he said.

Caroline walked into the room and narrowed her eyes as she viewed her mother and Joey suspiciously. "What are you talking about?" she asked.

"Joey just woke up and was telling me how he felt. He's a little better," Claire said.

"Good. He had me more than a little worried last night," Caroline said. "Caleb and I finally came to an agreement on which mares to breed with Leif. That man is the most bullheaded, opinionated person I have ever come across in all my life. And he knows that he is and enjoys it too. I think he takes pleasure in riling me up. Bringing him to the ranch may prove to be the worst thing Joey ever did to us."

Joey and Claire exchanged glances and he gave her a wink with his good eye.

Swinging his feet to the floor, Joey sat up and had to inhale deeply and slowly to ward of lightheadedness. He scrunched up his face from the pain in his side and he said, "Be nice to him. He's been through a lot. I guarantee you that he'll be there for you when you need him."

Ignoring her ranch foreman, Caroline said, "After I eat, I'm going to ride out and have another talk with the other ranchers. This business has to stop."

Joey took his fingers and felt his numb lips before speaking. "Caroline, don't do that. We are in a feud with somebody and you going to them will look like weakness. The only way to put a stop to this is to stand up to them. We just have to figure out which rancher we're dealing with," he said.

Caroline looked at her mother and then towards Joey. "Do you really think so?" she asked.

"I'm sure of it. A couple of us at a time need to go out to check on the mustangs and make a stand if we find trouble," Joey said.

"I hate this. All I want to do is run the ranch. I just don't understand people," Caroline said with exasperation.

"I fear my being gone put all this trouble into motion and I feel responsible. I truly am sorry. You know I'm not one for drama, but I believe we are at war," Joey said before reclining back onto the pillow and closing his eyes.

"Very well. You know I trust your wisdom. I'll send Dan and Bart out after lunch. You get some rest," Caroline said before leaving the room with her mother.

Claire cut some slices of bread from a loaf that she had made the day before while Caroline sliced the ham. They made sandwiches and took seats at the table.

The worry etched on her daughter's face, caught Claire's attention. "He looks rough, doesn't he?" she asked.

Caroline paused on raising the sandwich to her mouth. "He sure does. It about breaks my heart and makes me feel guilty for being mad at him for getting back here so late. Do you think he will recover?" she asked.

"Oh, I think so. He's a tough old bird, but he's not as young as he used to be. It's going to take some time," Claire replied.

"Mother, I don't know if I'm strong enough to handle all the trouble that may be headed our way," Caroline said.

"Sure you are. And except for maybe Bart, you can count on all the men to stand with you. They are a good bunch," Claire said.

"You have barely met Caleb. What makes you so sure about him?" Caroline asked.

"Lots of things. I watched him with Joey last night. He looked beside himself with worry. And maybe it's a mother's intuition, but I know a well-raised man when I see one. You need to be careful or you might start liking him," Claire said with a wizened smile.

"What is that supposed to mean?" Caroline asked.

"Oh, I think you'll figure it out soon," Claire said.

Caroline shook her head as if she were bewildered with her mother and took a bite of her sandwich to stifle any further discussion of the subject. They ate the rest of their meals while not straying from idle small talk. Caroline promptly headed back outside when she finished her last bite. She found Dan and Bart and gave them instructions to go check on the mustangs that they had turned back loose.

Dan and Bart were both grateful to get out from under the watchful eye of Caroline and to spend the rest of the day riding instead of working with horses. They mounted up and headed north towards the spots where they had rounded up the horses a couple of weeks earlier. As they came to a meadow between some foothills, they found a herd of cattle with Nathan Horn's brand on the animals. After riding around the herd, Dan and Bart cut through a pass that led to a lush valley with some of the best grass around anywhere. Trees lined the side of the basin and to get a look at the grasslands below them, the two men descended the side. At the bottom, they found a herd of mustangs. They recognized some of the horses as ones they had turned back out after the roundup. A stallion snorted and pawed the ground as he circled the herd. At the opposite end of the valley, a few hundred yards away, a herd of cattle crazed. The two ranch hands rode onto the grassland and eased around the herd with the intent to ride out the on the other side to look for more wild horses.

"Once we get out of here, we'll head east. I imagine we'll find some over in that direction. There's pretty good ..." Dan said before being interrupted by the roar of guns.

A volley of bullets kicked up dirt and grass in front of the two men's horses. Bart's horse reared up so suddenly that the ranch hand fell to the ground. He managed to hold on to one of the reins as he jumped to his feet. His horse frantically danced around him in a circle, pulling hard on the single rein. A second barrage of shots hit the ground even closer to their horse's feet and caused Bart's mount to kick out its rear legs high into the air. Dan moved his horse beside Bart's gelding and leaned over, grasping the bridle. His action gave Bart a moment to remount.

"Let's get out of here," Dan yelled.

Dan and Bart turned their horses and headed back from where they had come. The mustangs were running in every direction and the two men had to maneuver their horses as if on an obstacle course to keep from colliding with the startled animals. A final round of shots roared behind them just before they reached the cover of the trees.

Once they were back on top of the ridge, Dan stopped his horse. "Let's wait here a few minutes to listen if they shoot the mustangs," he said.

"I believe that was what you call tit for tat," Bart said.

"I'm surprised they didn't kill us after what they did to Joey. They could have hid our bodies and nobody would have ever found us," Dan said as he removed his hat and ran his fingers through his hair.

"Which ever rancher is behind this hasn't got quite brave enough to start killing yet or we'd be dead," Bart said.

After waiting a good fifteen minutes without hearing any more shots, the two ranch hands headed for home. They reached the ranch and saw Caroline, Caleb, and Scully moving the latest mares to foal into a separate pasture. When the trio rode back to the barn, Dan, talking a mile a minute in his excitement, reported what had happened to them.

The color drained from Caroline's face as she listened to Dan recount the events on their check on the mustangs. She felt at a loss on how to respond or what to do. As she looked around at the others, she found them all looking at her and waiting for a response that she didn't have.

Scully broke the silence. "Caroline, I think the world of you, but I've been part of these range wars before. I'm too old for this nonsense. I'd like my pay. Better to die a drunk than by a bullet," he said.

"But you have been doing so well. Are you sure this is what you want?" Caroline asked.

The old man didn't answer, but looked Caroline in the eye with a gaze that didn't falter.

"Very well, let's head to the house. Caleb, would use please accompany us? I'm sure Joey would like to see you," Caroline said before turning towards her home.

As she walked with the two men, she wondered if asking Caleb to accompany her had sounded lame. She didn't want to offend Dan and Bart since they had known Joey a lot longer than Caleb had, but the truth of the matter was that Caleb had fighting experience and the others did not. The notion that she needed her new ranch hand's expertise irked her to no end, but she had no intention of letting pride be the root of the ranch's demise.

Inside the home, Caroline walked to the office and retrieved money from the safe. She paid Scully for a whole month of wages as if he had worked the total time. Even though she found his choice of returning to the bottle to be sad and pitiful, she gave the old man a hug and wished him well. Scully gazed at her as if he were seeing Caroline for the last time before thanking her and taking his leave.

Caroline led Caleb to the spare bedroom and found it empty. With a puzzled look, she headed to the kitchen. She found Joey at the table eating soup with her mother sitting across from him. Once again, she noticed a coziness between the two of them that didn't sit well with her. She had no qualms that Joey was of high enough character for her mother, but the notion of somebody replacing her daddy made her feel physically weak.

"What's going on?" Claire asked when she looked up at the sound of Caroline and Caleb entering the room looking glum.

"Dan and Bart were fired upon. Apparently, the culprits had no intention of hitting them. Unfortunately, Dan and Bart never felt like they could make a stand. They headed back here without returning fire or seeing anyone. We obviously have problems," Caroline said.

"Maybe we need to go talk to Colonel Devin. I realize that he hasn't been at Fort Laramie for very long and that we don't know him well, but maybe he can help," Claire said.

Joey set his spoon down and looked up at the others. "I don't think we can count on the army. They have their hands full keeping an eye on the Indians and we haven't had any real trouble yet. That's the problem when you live somewhere where you have to depend on the army for law and order. I don't think me taking a beating outside of a saloon will impress him much," he said.

"What do we do then?" Caroline asked.

"Unless Caleb has a better idea, I think we do just what we did today, but maybe be a little more careful. The next time we need to engage them in a battle. I know it's not what any of us want, but I believe we have to take a stand," Joey said.

All eyes turned to Caleb and he realized that they were waiting for him to speak. Getting asked to help make such dire decisions after only two days on the job made him uncomfortable. He tried to think quickly of alternatives to Joey's suggestion as the others waited for him to speak. "I don't know what else we can do right now. We need to know our enemy before we can do much else. Maybe we need a couple more men and start doing a night watch," he said.

"Scully quit so I can replace him and I guess we can afford one more. I'll hire Lucky and Reese back if they are interested. Both are pretty good men. I don't know how handy they are with a gun though," Caroline said.

"They're as good as anybody else you'll find unemployed. I meant to tell you that Frankie Myers was in the saloon last night running his mouth. He and his outfit left before I did and I wouldn't be surprised if they were the ones that jumped me," Joey offered.

"I guess it is settled then, but I sure wish Daddy were here," Caroline said as she put her hat back on and looked at her mother.

As Caleb walked outside with Caroline, he said, "If you don't mind, I think I'll get Dan and Bart and do a little target shooting. It never hurts to know how good of a shot they are and the practice will do them good."

"Do you think there is going to be bloodshed?" Caroline asked.

"It never hurts to be prepared," he said.

"And I take it that you always are," she said.

Caleb mind flashed to the scene of riding up on Charles asleep on the veranda. If he hadn't let anger get the better of him, he wouldn't have ridden up on his brother-in-law so carelessly with no plan other than to beat the snot out of Charles. With a little preparation, he would still live in Tennessee and Charles would be alive. Choosing his words carefully, he said, "Fighting in a war will teach you to be prepared. It can be the difference between life and death. I try not to have to relearn that very often."

"I'll grab my rifle. It would be good for me to take a few shots. After that, I'm headed to town to see if I can hire Reese and Lucky again," Caroline said.

"It'll be dark by the time you get back," Caleb said.

"I'm a big girl and the dark doesn't frighten me. I'll be fine," she said.

"I'm going with you. Things are different now. Joey wanted me to go with him last night and I didn't feel like riding. He probably wouldn't be in the shape he's in if I'd gone. I not going to make the same mistake twice," he said.

"You do know that you work for me, don't you? I make the decisions around here," Caroline said testily.

"I insist on going," Caleb said defiantly.

"Mr. Gunnar, I don't owe you a thing. I could fire you right now," she said.

"Listen, I know this is your ranch, but can't we quit butting heads on everything. I think me accompanying you is in the best interest of everybody," he said as he looked down into Caroline's eyes.

Caroline met his gaze head on. He looked so sincere and noble that she wanted to slap him and slap Joey for bringing Caleb to the ranch. She could feel herself begin to waffle and clenched her jaw in an attempt not to frown. Taking a big breath, she exhaled loudly. "Very well, but I find your brazenness grating. We will quit butting heads when you quit expressing your opinions so freely. Let's go shoot," she said before walking off to retrieve her rifle.

"You probably should be the one to tell Dan and Bart so that they don't think I'm bossing them," Caleb called out.

Looking over her shoulder, Caroline said, "I wish you respected my feelings as much as you do theirs."

Caleb found four empty feed sacks in the barn and used axle grease to make a target spot on each one. He then dumped some empty bean cans from the bunkhouse trash into a fifth sack and headed out to the rail fence to tack up the sacks so that the shots would not be towards the horses. By that time, Caroline, Dan, and Bart stood waiting with their rifles. Walking back to the group, Caleb took his place in line.

"How about seven shots apiece?" Caroline suggested.

The four of them raised their rifles and commenced shooting at the same time. By the time they finished firing the guns, a cloud of black powder smoke hung around them in the still air like a fog. Caleb had always prided himself in his marksmanship with a rifle and had to stymie a grin when the targets revealed he had done the best. Both Caroline and Bart had done well and even Dan's shooting proved accurate enough to put a man down.

"I'd say we'd make a formidable army," Caleb remarked.

"Just remember that the next time you irritate me," Caroline said with an impish smile.

As Caleb looked in her direction, he wasn't sure if the grin was an attempt at humor or maybe laced with malevolence. "I'll keep that in mind," he said as he retrieved cans from the sack and set them on the fence.

"I don't shoot pistols. I'm going to go to the house," Caroline said and walked off towards the barn.

Dan and Bart didn't attempt to draw their guns to fire, but instead took careful aim before shooting. Neither cowboy proved much of a shot with a revolver. Bart took out a chunk of fence directly below a can to send it toppling and Dan knocked one can down. Caleb waited until the others had finished. He took a breath and reminded himself not to rush his draw - accuracy over speed. Wiggling his fingers a couple of times, Caleb smoothly drew his Colt and rapidly fired off six shots. Four cans flew through the air.

"Nice shooting," Dan said.

"I wish I would've hit all of them," Caleb lamented.

"I'm betting those two you missed would be hurting real bad if they were men," Dan said.

"Let's hope so," Caleb said as they headed towards the bunkhouse, reloading their guns as they walked.

"So do you think Joey is going to be okay?" Dan asked.

"Oh, sure. He just needs time to heal," Caleb said before wondering if Dan and Bart might feel slighted for not getting to visit the ranch foreman. "Listen, the only reason that I got invited in is that I have fighting experience and they wanted my opinion on the troubles around here. I sure wouldn't win any popularity contest with Caroline."

Dan nodded his head and Bart didn't seem to be listening to the conversation.

Caroline stood waiting at the barn with her and Caleb's horses. "Are you ready to head to town?" she asked Caleb.

"Aren't we going to eat before we leave?" Caleb asked.

"The sooner we leave, the sooner we get back," Caroline replied.

Caleb climbed aboard his horse without saying another word and they started riding towards town.

Once they reached the road, Caroline looked over and said, "Mother and Joey approved of your chivalry in accompanying me."

"I'm not sure I'd call it chivalry. I think a guilty conscience for Joey getting beat up is probably more accurate," Caleb noted.

"Joey probably realizes that, but believe me, Mother would refuse to consider it anything other than chivalry. By the way, Joey suggested we dine at the hotel. He thought it would be good for others to see that the ranch has some new men. I didn't want Dan and Bart to feel slighted. I've never dined in town with them," she said.

"I'm sure you wished likewise concerning me," Caleb said with a grin.

"As long as you don't slurp or chew with your mouth open, I think I'll survive," Caroline responded.

"Not with how my momma raised me," he said.

"Good to know," Caroline said matter-of-factly.

With a wry smile, Caleb said, "Joey keeps singing your praises. I personally just don't see it. I'm not sure why you find me so repulsive. I had a reputation for being well liked in my community and Robin and I were certainly happy together. I made a pretty fair husband."

"I can assure you that I'm not looking for a husband. And while on the subject, my former husband was a whore mongering fool. Maybe he soured me on all men," she said.

"I certainly wasn't suggesting a marriage. My point being that there once was a young woman that didn't find me so egregious. I truly am sorry that your marriage didn't work out so well," he said.

"To show I can be nice, I will say that I appreciate your vocabulary. You use words that I do not often hear around here. Now let's drop the subject," Caroline said.

The two rode on in silence for a couple of miles before Caroline began talking about her plans for the ranch to break the silence. Caleb listened intently and gave approval of her ideas, but never dared to make any suggestions. They rode up to the Fort Laramie Hotel and went inside to the dining area. Both ordered beefsteaks served with potatoes and greens.

Some area ranchers sat around dining. Thomas Rhodes and Nathan Horn had a table in the corner and Caroline pointed out that she suspected one or both of them to be the culprits behind her ranch's recent troubles. A couple of other area ranchers walked over to say hello to Caroline. Even in men's clothing, she obviously had her admirers. She politely greeted the men and introduced Caleb as the ranch's new horseman.

Rhodes and Horn stopped at Caroline's table on their way out of the dining hall.

"Have you had any more trouble?" Nathan asked.

"Somebody beat Joey up last night outside the saloon," Caroline said coolly.

"I heard about that," Thomas said.

"Well, if you did then you must have gotten it straight from the horse's mouth because nobody else knows about it," Caroline said.

Nathan gave Thomas a dirty look and the two men walked away without saying another word.

"That pretty much proves your theory correct on the source of your problems," Caleb said.

"Yes, it does. I just wish I knew which one of them it is or if they are in cahoots," she said.

After finishing their meals, Caroline insisted on paying the tab, much to the chagrin of Caleb. He found himself baffled by her need to always be in control of every situation and wished that for just one moment that she would let up on her obsession with being in charge of the ranch.

They strolled down the boardwalk to the Fort Laramie Saloon as the sun began sinking below the horizon,

"I hope Lucky and Reese are in there so that we can get back home. I don't cherish the notion of having to wait around town," Caroline said before marching into the saloon.

As her eyes adjusted to the dim light and smoke, Caroline scanned the bar patrons. She saw Lucky and Reese sitting at a table towards the back and Frankie Myers and two other men sitting at a table near the bar.

"Well, if it isn't Puss in Boots. Looks like she has her a new beau to replace Joey. I wonder if Joey isn't feeling so well," Frankie said and let out a cackle.

Caleb's temples began pulsating as he tensed his muscles and gritted his teeth. The rage he had never quite learned to harness was ready to explode. He raised his leg and drove his boot into the edge of the tabletop. The table caught Frankie in the chest and sent him and his chair toppling over backwards with a crash that silenced the saloon's patrons and turned all eyes towards the noise. Caleb stood with his fists clenched at his sides waiting for Frankie to stand. The two men sitting with Frankie jumped up and rushed Caleb, grabbing him by the arms. Frankie took a moment to get to his feet and then flipped the table out of his way as he charged. With a deft swing of his leg, Caleb kicked Frankie in the groin. The cowboy dropped as if he were brought down with a buffalo gun.

Mayhem had broken out so fast that Caroline could barely fathom what had happened. She realized that Caleb still needed help. With a grab of the nearest beer mug on the bar, she swung it for all she was worth into the temple of the nearest man holding Caleb. As the cowboy dropped to the floor, Caleb used his freed arm to pummel the other ranch hand into submission.

"He's reaching for his gun," Caroline screamed.

With cat like reflexes, Caleb drove his boot heel into the back of Frankie's hand. The cowboy let out a scream that made patrons wince in discomfort.

As Caleb drew his revolver, he yelled, "I'm tired and my hand hurts. The next man than steps my way is going to die."

The bar grew deathly still as the patrons stared at the unfamiliar young man with the veins bulging in his neck.

Caroline decided to use the moment to conduct her business. She barked out in her take-charge manner, "Lucky and Reese, you need to come with us. You now work for the Langley Ranch."

The two cowboys, used to taking orders, got up from their seats and walked over as if they never had a decision to make in the matter.

"Let's get out of here," Caleb said as he began stepping backwards with his gun still drawn.

As the four of them headed back towards the ranch, Caroline said, "You have a bit of temper there, don't you?"

"Where I come from, you don't insult ladies and you don't joke about bushwhacking my friend. And by the way, thank you for your help. I was in a bit of a pickle," Caleb said.

"So, even with your lowly opinion of me, you still consider me a lady?" Caroline asked with a grin that Caleb could just barely see in the fading light.

"Only in the very broadest sense of the word," he replied with a devilish smile.

Chapter 15

After eating breakfast with the other ranch hands, Caleb walked to the barn and saddled his mount. He had taken a shine to the horse that he and Joey had bartered for on the trail. Joey had made no attempt to sell the animal and Caleb admired its surefootedness. While deciding that the horse needed a name, Caleb had started calling it Traveler. He still planned to make Diablo his everyday mount, but that horse was still a work in progress and had a ways to go before he trusted the spirited animal.

As Caleb walked out of the barn with Traveler in tow, he saw the man that Caroline had pointed out as Nathan Horn lope his horse into the yard and march onto the porch like a mad Banty rooster. Nathan pounded on the door so hard that the sound carried clear to the barn. With his curiosity aroused, Caleb watched as the rancher stood impatiently waiting for someone to come greet him.

Alarmed by the beating on the door, Caroline and Claire had both scuttled to the entrance. The sight of Nathan Horn had taken them both by surprise. His red face and scowl left no doubt that the man wasn't there for a social visit.

"Nathan, come on in," Claire said as she and Caroline stepped out of the way to allow the rancher into their home. "What brings you here?"

Yanking his hat from his head, Nathan ranted, "Caroline knows full well why I'm here. She and her new cowboy put three of my ranch hands out of work. Frankie's hand is broken and might never be the same. Eddie's nose is busted and his eyes are black and he's so sore he can't get out of bed. And Caroline is lucky that she didn't kill Candy when she hit him upside the head with that beer mug. He can't stand to open his eyes because the light hurts him so bad. I've come to demand restitution for my losses."

Claire's mouth remained gapped open in surprise after hearing Nathan's tirade- an act she would have found most unladylike under normal circumstances. As she looked over at her daughter, she said in an ironic voice, "I guess this didn't cross your mind as newsworthy this morning."

Caroline put her hands on her hips and tried to make herself look tall. "Frankie should have kept his big mouth shut if he didn't want somebody to shut it for him. He insulted me and practically confessed to beating Joey. Since he works for you, and Thomas already knew about the beating, I'd say that makes you suspect for being involved in the whole thing so I'd change my tone if I were you. As for my part in last night, I was merely evening the odds a little," she said defiantly.

"I never ordered anybody to rough up Joey," Nathan yelled.

"You and Thomas certainly didn't seem too distraught about it last night," Caroline responded.

"I'm a rancher, not a wet nurse," Nathan replied.

"But you did have your men kill the mustangs, didn't you? Now your ranch hands think they can get by with anything," Caroline accused.

"I don't answer to no woman and I've not broken any laws," Nathan countered.

"And I don't know why you came here. You know we have no intention of paying you. You just wanted to come yell," Caroline said.

"You do a lot of barking for someone so small. I doubt you have much bite," Nathan challenged.

"Candy might argue otherwise and you might be the next one to find out," Caroline yelled.

Claire stepped between her daughter and Nathan. "Nathan, this all needs to stop before somebody gets killed. We will leave you and your men alone. You need to do likewise and leave the mustangs alone. They are our livelihood and there is plenty of land to go around for all of us," she said.

"My son is of the age to start his own ranch. Milo and I just might want to have us a cattle empire and control the whole north side of Fort Laramie," Nathan said.

"Please stop this before somebody gets killed," Claire pleaded.

With a scowl on his face, Nathan said, "I'm not sure Frankie and the rest of the boys will be willing to let this go."

"You are their boss. I suggest that you make them. Think about what I said about ending this before it's too late. Now you need to go," Claire said.

The rancher stood there eyeing the two women. His contempt was palpable. Nathan seemed at a loss for words, but unwilling to leave on the demands of Claire.

Joey slipped into the room. "Mr. Horn, you need to leave now," he said.

Nathan looked towards the doorway in surprise at seeing Joey recuperating in the house. "Like you are in any shape to make me leave," he said.

"I'll ask you nicely one more time to leave," Joey warned.

"Go to hell," Nathan said.

Reaching back for the buffet in the adjoining room, Joey grabbed the revolver that he had set there. He didn't point it at the rancher, but instead rested it against his chest and stared at the rancher.

"You'll all be sorry," Nathan shouted before marching out the door.

Claire turned towards her daughter and gave her an inquisitive look. Joey walked up to the young woman and did the same.

"What are you two looking at?" Caroline asked with mock ignorance.

"You know darn well what we're looking at. What happened last night and why didn't you tell me?" Claire asked.

"Caleb and I went into the saloon to find Lucky and Reese. As soon as we walked in, Frankie called me a most unladylike name and mouthed off about wondering if Joey didn't feel good. The next thing I know, Caleb is sending Frankie crashing to the floor. The other two men with Frankie grabbed Caleb by the arms so I laid a mug upside one cowboy's head. Caleb took care of it from there. Our Mr. Gunnar has quite the temper. It flows as quickly as his opinions. He is like a crazed man when he's mad. One more reason I question the wisdom of having him on the ranch," Caroline said in a tone a little too awestruck to match her criticism of Caleb or quite hide her beaming pride in the previous night's events.

"You don't sound too terribly upset with Caleb to me," Joey noted.

"Well, he was defending my and your honor. You could say that is an admirable trait even if his quick temper is alarming," Caroline offered.

"Why didn't you tell me at breakfast?" Claire asked.

"I didn't think my mother would be too happy to learn first thing in the morning that her daughter had been in a bar fight," Caroline answered.

"I see," Claire said skeptically.

"The whole thing happened so fast," Caroline added for further justification.

Claire turned towards Joey as he worked to stifle a grin. "Joey, I think you better go fire Caleb. I agree with Caroline that his being here may not be wise."

"Yeah, we better break up Caleb and Caroline before they start robbing banks together or something. They are beginning to sound like a pair. As much as they claim to dislike each other, I wouldn't have thought he would defend her honor or that she would take up fighting for him," Joey said.

"Well, it supposedly happened very fast. Maybe neither of them had time to think on whom they were helping," Claire said in a satirical voice.

Caroline leaned back and folded her arms as she realized that she was being teased. "You both may think this is all funny, but we have troubles on our hands. More so than ever after last night. We need to come up with a plan and quit wasting time," she said.

"Yes, dear, you are right. You and Caleb could have been hurt last night. As soon as you admit that Caleb is not half as bad as you let on, we'll get to business," Claire said.

Both her mother and Joey were smirking at her. Caroline couldn't fathom what all the fuss was over with the two of them. She wondered if they both thought that they were cupid or something. "Listen, I will admit that it was exciting to have someone so readily stand up for me last night. My ex-husband certainly never would have, but let's not make more out of it than it is. I think it had more to do with all his southern gentleman nonsense than it did me. There are times when Caleb's intelligence and character make him enjoyable to be around, but most of the time he's too hardheaded and full of his opinions to suit me. Regardless, I have made it quite clear on how I feel about ever having a man in my life again. That ship has done sailed. Now can we move on?" she said.

"I guess there's only room for one hardhead on this ranch," Claire mused. "Why don't you go get Caleb so the four of us can figure this out?"

Not wishing to debate the subject any further, Caroline headed out the door.

"I'm not sure if those two are made for each other or one of them will kill the other. The sparks sure fly when they're together," Joey mused.

Claire chuckled. "Her first idiot husband has soured Caroline on men or at least she thinks so, but I can see her eyes twinkle even when she's disparaging Caleb. I think she actually believes what she's telling us. Her head and her heart just aren't on the same page. You've done a lot for this ranch over the years, but bringing Caleb here might prove to be the best thing you ever did for us. Let's just hope we all live through what's about to come our way."

Chapter 16

Four days had passed since Nathan Horn had made his unannounced visit to the Langley home. Everybody at the ranch kept waiting for trouble to start at any moment, but nothing had happened so far. All of them were tired and grouchy from night watches, checking on the mustangs, and breaking the young horses. Lucky and Reese were adequate at their jobs at best and the extra responsibilities had everyone stretched thin.

Joey's head injury symptoms had passed except for a sore spot on the back of his head. The swelling had gone out of his black eye, but his ribs remained so tender that he still walked around like an old man. He felt as if he had overstayed his welcome in the Langley home, but failed in his effort to return to the bunkhouse. Claire would not hear of him leaving, insisting that she knew he would attempt to work, and risk further injury.

As Caroline ate breakfast with her mother and Joey, she covertly watched the two of them. The ease in which they interacted with each other reminded Caroline of her mother with her daddy. She found the similarities troubling. To her way of thinking, no one could measure up to her father. Joey was a good and loyal employee, but the lifelong bachelor had nothing to show for his labors. She could clearly see that her mother was attracted to Joey and wondered why. Did her mother need a man in her life that badly? How could anyone replace her daddy? The sight of the two of them together produced so many questions in Caroline's mind. She hurriedly finished her meal, said goodbye, and walked outside feeling upset and hurt.

She and Caleb were supposed to ride out to keep an eye on the mustangs that morning. As she walked into the barn, Caroline found Caleb's horse saddled and Caleb tightening the cinch on her gelding.

"Do I need to double check it?" Caroline asked sarcastically.

"Nah, I wouldn't have anybody to argue with if something were to happen to you," Caleb responded.

Letting out a scoff, Caroline said, "I'm sure with your disposition that you would find a replacement rather quickly."

The two rode out in the direction of the foothills. Caleb sensed Caroline's ill mood and didn't bother to attempt a conversation. As he gazed off towards the mountains that he still found awe inspiring, he felt content to be outside on a beautiful day. The temperature seemed perfect for riding and the bright sunshine gave the landscape a nice glow. He had no intention of letting Caroline's mood ruin his day.

Out of the blue, Caroline said, "You should see Mother and Joey at the breakfast table. You would think they were married or something. I don't know what Mother is thinking."

The serenity that Caleb had enjoyed shattered like a whiskey bottle hurled against a rock. He looked over at Caroline and shook his head. "I realize that none of us can see our parents as anything but old, but your mother is no such thing. And there's more to her than just being your mother. She has a lot of life still to live and I could see why she wouldn't want to do it alone," he said.

"I will always be with her to keep her company," she said.

"Caroline, you don't know that. Staying mad at all of us men for another fifty or sixty years is a long time. Frankie

Myers might have a change of heart and come apologize to you and you could be smitten," Caleb joked.

Making a derisive snorting sound before speaking, Caroline said, "I'd even take you over Frankie. I know that Joey is a fine man, but I still don't think it would look proper for a ranch owner to take up with one of her cowboys."

"Are you sure you're not imagining things?" he asked.

"I don't think so. They act so natural together. Just like a couple that has been together forever," she said.

"As far as Joey goes, not every man wants to admit it, but luck plays an awfully big part of his success. Some are born into the right family, or happen to be at the right place at the right time, or maybe marry the right woman to help him along the way. I don't think Joey ever had much luck as far as I can tell. That doesn't make him any lesser of a man," Caleb said.

Caroline sighed. "You can say whatever you want, but you are not going to change my mind. I don't like it and I think it's a lot of nonsense," she said in a voice more petulant child than grown woman.

Clenching his teeth, Caleb attempted to stay quiet, but his tongue lost the battle with his anger. "That's because you are a self-centered, conceited brat. Sometimes your facial expressions look just like a spoiled little child. And you think of no one but yourself. Grow up and let your momma be happy. Someone in your family needs to be," he yelled.

"Of course, you have an opinion on everything and know more than anyone. I never asked you what you thought," she yelled back.

"Then why did you bring up the subject?" Caleb demanded.

"For all you know, Joey might be taking up with Mother just to get control of the ranch," Caroline speculated.

Caleb pulled his horse to a stop and took a big breath, exhaling slowly. He really did like Caroline and had come to understand Joey's fondness for her. Under all her anger, he could occasionally see the person that she had once been and he understood full well how life could change you in ways that you didn't ask for or want. But he drew the line when it came to disparaging his friend. "I need to know right now if you were just being childish or if you really meant what you just suggested," he said in a flat monotone voice.

As Caroline stopped her horse, she turned to look at Caleb. She expected to see his face scrunched in anger, but was surprised to see that he looked tired and as if he had just lost his best friend. His expression made her instantly feel guilty and recognize that she had gone too far with her tirade. She also realized that Caleb had again pinned her into a corner - either admit to being childish or confess that she had meant what she had said. As she looked Caleb in the eye, she could see that her reply would determine if he stayed or quit the ranch. There would be no saving face if she wanted him to remain, and for reasons she couldn't quite grasp, the thought of him leaving made her feel panicky. "I was being childish. Joey is as noble and honest as they come. I'm sorry I upset you," she said meekly.

"Good. I can live with that," he said. His momma had always stressed giving forgiveness when it is sought and the act came naturally to him now without thought. He nudged his horse into moving without saying another word.

They rode on for a half-hour without speaking. The silence killed Caroline. She needed to hear Caleb talk to see if he had any lingering resentment. "I can't seem to get over my bitterness for my failed marriage. Don't you ever feel bitter that your wife and baby died?" she asked.

Caleb looked at her thoughtfully as he contemplated his answer. "I was very bitter for the first year or so. After a while, I guess the finality of it set in and I accepted that they were gone. Then things felt more like a bad scar that will always show. I wear it every day and know I'm not the same person I once was," he said.

"I can't seem to get past the bitter part. I felt so much humiliation that my husband ran off with a jezebel. It didn't do much for how I felt about myself," Caroline said.

"I can understand that. Embarrassment can have a powerful hold on people. My little sister got laughed at one time in church while stumbling through reading a Bible verse. To this day, she doesn't like to read because of one silly moment with some rotten kids. Only thing I can tell you is that people forget the past if you let them. Going around mad at the world just serves to remind folks of what you used to be like and why you are the way that you are now," Caleb said.

Smiling, Caroline said, "I should have known that you would have an opinion on that too. I'll keep what you said in mind though. It's probably the first thing that you have said that I might agree with."

"I guess that's a start," he said and smiled.

Caroline led Caleb to the overlook where she and the other ranch hands had fired at the men chasing the mustangs before Caleb had arrived. They took seats on rocks and watched a herd of mustangs grazing down below them. Three mares that had foaled and been bred back before being turned loose had rejoined the other horses. The foals frolicked about chasing each other.

As Caroline turned to look at Caleb, she asked, "Do you think you will ever have children again?"

While not taking his eyes off the foals down below them, Caleb said, "I don't really know. I guess I might ought to worry about ever having a wife again first thing, but with what I've been through, I think I would be a tad gun shy. And besides, with your lowly opinion of me, I'm thinking I got lucky to ever have found a wife the first time. What about you?"

Letting out a chuckle, Caroline picked up a rock and began rubbing it. "I certainly thought so at one time, but with my lowly opinion of all you men, I find that highly unlikely," she said.

"You're casting an awfully big net when you throw us all in together," he said.

"I suppose so. Life would be a lot easier if it were possible to know what really went on inside of people's heads," Caroline said.

"What would be the fun in that? Life needs a little mystery. Kind of like salt and pepper for a little seasoning," Caleb said.

"Maybe, but I'm apparently not very good at solving life's riddles. I guess I like things bland. We better go do some more riding," she said as she stood and brushed the dust off her pants.

Caleb tried not to watch, but found he couldn't take his eyes off Caroline's rear. Even dressed in her men's clothing, there was no denying that Caroline was fine looking. He hadn't been with a woman since the death of Robin and the loneliness and aching need for one bubbled to the surface, making him feel as empty as a hollowed out tree. Caroline looked up and caught him watching her. With a quick turn, Caleb mounted his horse and looked towards the horizon.

While riding for the rest of the morning, they didn't find any more mustangs or see a soul. Towards noon, they came upon a small stream with some shade provided by pine trees. They decided to stop for lunch. Caroline reached into her saddlebag to retrieve some sandwiches stuffed with boiled ham that Claire had made for them.

The awkward moment they shared at the rocks had passed as they sat down and began talking about their expectations for the foals that Leif would sire next spring. Caleb had just taken a big hunk out of his sandwich and was chewing away when multiple gunshots rang out in the distance. He spit out his bite of food and rushed to his horse with Caroline at his heels doing to the same.

"Follow me, I think I've got a pretty good idea from where that's coming," Caroline yelled as she heeled her horse into a lope.

Caroline headed along the stream before cutting left through a trail between the foothills. Shots continued to ring out as they rode and she tried to determine the direction in which the shooters appeared to be moving. She remembered a plateau and guessed that some riders could be driving mustangs through the pass. Cutting her horse to the right between some more hills, she and Caleb raced towards the gunfire. As they reached the plateau, mustangs were charging towards them from the left with three riders in pursuit.

"There's a cliff a half-mile or so from here. I think they're planning on running them off of it," Caroline yelled as she pulled her rifle from her scabbard.

"Get behind those rocks. I'm riding out there to stop them," Caleb yelled.

"They won't stop. They'll kill you," she warned.

"We can't just murder them and we have to do something. If they fire on me, let them have it. I'll approach at an angle so they won't have much of a shot," Caleb shouted as he retrieved his Winchester rifle.

As the mustangs passed by them, Caleb spurred his mount into a gallop between the shooters and the wild horses. He swung his arm wildly in an attempt to wave the men off from their charge while keeping a keen eye out for the rider's next move. Two of the men lowered their revolvers from pointing towards the sky. They took aim at Caleb.

"Here we go," Caleb said to himself.

Caleb bent behind his horse's neck, trying to make himself as small of a target as possible. The two revolvers fired one after the other and were answered immediately by the crack of a rifle. Caleb popped his head up to see the man farthest to his left fall from the saddle. As Caleb turned his horse straight into the path of the nearest gunman, he reminded himself of his cavalry training as he smoothly raised his rifle and took aim. The man was now no farther than thirty yards away with eyes wide with surprise, desperately trying to aim his gun as Caleb's shot tore into his chest. Knocked back onto the horse's rump by the force of the bullet, the rider flopped around wildly as the animal bucked until the man catapulted through the air. Another shot from Caroline missed the third man, but proved enough of a threat to make the rider turn his horse around and race away. Caleb contemplated pursuing the escaping man, but didn't have the stomach for another killing. He turned his horse and trotted back to Caroline.

"I've never killed anybody before," Caroline said as if talking to herself as she walked out to meet Caleb.

Caroline looked as pale as a ghost and Caleb could see her shoulder's trembling. She set her rifle against a rock and stood there looking pitiful and on the verge of tears. Climbing down from his horse, Caleb walked over and embraced her. He wondered if the gesture might upset her further, but Caroline buried her head against his chest and began crying.

"We did what we had to do," Caleb said as he patted her back. Seeing Caroline in such a vulnerable state seemed a little startling to his senses. He truly felt compassion for what she had gone through and did his best to comfort her with soothing words.

She didn't speak until she had cried herself out. "We saved the horses, but I fear what we've unleashed now," she said.

"We better head home," Caleb said as he removed his arms from around Caroline and stood there awkwardly waiting for her to do the same.

As she stepped back, Caroline took her hands and wiped the tears from her eyes. "I bet you never saw a ranch owner cry. I'm sorry," she said.

"I'd be worried about you if you didn't shed some tears. Killing still bothers me and I fought in a war. I've seen enough death to last a lifetime. There's something wrong with a person if they ever get used to it. The one I shot was the one that you laid the beer mug upside his head. I guess if we had any lingering doubt that we now know it's Nathan for sure," he said.

"Nathan called him Candy. I didn't recognize the man that I shot," she added.

"Well, we best not dally," Caleb said before turning to grab the reins to his horse.

"Caleb, thank you for comforting me," Caroline said before quickly walking away to retrieve her horse.

Chapter 17

By the time that Caleb and Caroline made it back to the ranch after the shootings, the enormity of Caroline's actions were again weighing heavily on her. She marched straight into her room and dropped onto her bed, leaving Caleb to recount what had happened. Claire and Joey stared at him in confusion over Caroline's unusual behavior. Caleb dreaded being the one to break the news on what had happened and pulled his hat off and cleared his throat. As he recounted what had happened, he thought that Claire looked as if she might wilt upon hearing of the killings and the fact that her daughter had taken a life. She stood as if frozen with her trembling hands pressed against her mouth. Joey paced about the room, holding his side as he walked.

Joey stopped and turned towards the others. "I guess we knew we were headed towards this. Better them than one of us," he said.

"This is terrible. I don't understand what Nathan can be thinking. Does he really see us as that much of a threat? And I feel for Caleb and Caroline. No sooner than Caleb arrives here and he is in a war. And no woman should have to be out killing folks," Claire said.

"What do you think we next need to do?" Caleb asked.

"Everybody, including me, needs to be on guard tonight. We'll make a perimeter around the house and the bunkhouse. I don't know if they'll retaliate that quickly, but we need to be prepared," Joey said.

"How many men work for Nathan?" Caleb asked.

"Usually, about seven. I guess they're down to five now, but we can't assume that Thomas and his men aren't in on this too," Joey warned.

Claire grasped the sleeve of Joey's shirt. "You have no business leaving the house. You can't even walk without holding your side," she said.

As Caleb watched the interaction between Joey and Claire, he realized that Caroline hadn't exaggerated about the developing bond between the two of them.

"I don't plan to be walking. I'll be sitting and keep an eye on things," Joey replied.

"But what if you need to run?" Claire asked.

"Claire, if I don't help, and we get overrun, I'd be running anyways. I'll be fine," Joey assured her.

"I suppose," Claire said doubtfully. "I guess I better go talk to Caroline and see how she is doing."

"Ma'am, I could go check on her if you don't mind," Caleb offered. "I feel kind of responsible for today."

Barely hiding her surprise, Claire said, "By all means, if you think you can help her."

As Caleb walked towards the bedroom, Joey stretched his face in an intentionally exaggerated display of surprise and held out his hands palm up in answer to Claire's inquisitive look.

Caleb knocked on the door to Caroline's bedroom.

"Come in," she hollered.

As Caleb walked into the room for the first time, he said, "Hey, how are you doing?"

At the sound of his voice, Caroline turned her head towards the door with a look of surprise on her face. "Oh, I was expecting Mother," she said. "I guess I'm doing all right."

"I just wanted to check. Caroline, we had to save the mustangs and we attempted to stop those men peacefully. They shot first. We had a choice to fight or die. Sometimes things come down to that. Believe me, I know whence I speak, but that's a story for a different day. The next time you get upset just remind yourself that you had no other option but to fight. Of course, maybe you're just sad that you didn't let them finish me off so that you'd be rid of me for once and for all," Caleb said in an attempt at humor.

Attempting a smile, Caroline said, "And what would I do without all your, shall we say, guidance?"

"Keep on bossing everybody I suppose," he said and grinned.

Sitting up on her bed, Caroline swung her feet to the floor. "Caleb, what do you think next happens?"

"I don't know. Joey wants us to stand guard tonight," he said.

Caroline reached for her boots and pulled them onto her feet. "Let's go hear Joey's plan. This isn't the time for me to lie around feeling sorry for myself," she said as she stood and headed for the door.

Joey tried to talk Caroline into not taking part in the guard duty but failed in deterring her. He and Caleb began walking a circle around the buildings to pick out seven hiding spots to station each person.

"I take it that you and our boss came to some kind of understanding today," Joey said.

Caleb smiled. "Don't ask me. We definitely had some highs and lows on our ride. By tomorrow, she may not have any use for me again," he said.

"I doubt that after she let you into her room and you were able to talk to her. A day ago she would have had a fit if you tried something like that," Joey said, giving Caleb a wink.

"That is one little complicated woman. I do see what you meant when you said that there's a good side to her. She just has a tendency to let her bitterness get the best of her way too often," Caleb said.

"Tendency, huh? Is that what you call it? I'm going to start learning big words if I hang around you too much. So do you have a tendency to think that she's one fine little woman?" Joey asked before stopping to catch his breath.

Letting out a snort, Caleb said, "I think you're imagining things now."

"I may be a lifelong bachelor, but I know a thing or two about the matters of the heart. I see how you two act around each other. Your and her eyes light up when you're together - even when you both pretend you can't stand each other," Joey said.

"I can see too. You better concern yourself with whether you'll be Caroline's second victim when she decides you're going to be her stepdaddy," Caleb warned.

"Now I think you must have been the one that got hit in the head instead of me," Joey said before he resumed walking, changing the subject to finding another suitable hiding place.

By the time the two men completed the circuit, Joey ambled with a labored step, his face was beaded with sweat, and his brow furrowed in pain. As he presented his plan, Caroline offered no resistance or made any suggestions. Bart and Lucky stood and listened with obvious looks of disdain for the task until Joey dressed them down.

Once Joey finished talking, he and Caroline returned to the house for dinner while Caleb and the rest of the crew walked to the bunkhouse to begin fixing their meal. Caleb expected grumblings at the table about standing guard through the night or the fact that Joey was still staying at the house, but if anybody thought such things, they kept their opinions to themselves.

As dusk settled over the land, everyone grabbed a box of cartridges and their rifle before heading to their assigned spot. The air cooled with the darkness, making staying awake an easy proposition, and caused the group to continuously blow hot air into their hands to keep their fingers from growing stiff. Time seemed to drag at a snail's pace and the new moon made checking a pocket watch impossible without striking a match.

Sometime after two in the morning, the roar of Bart's Winchester shattered the stillness of the night. Joey had given instructions that only the people on either side of a shooter were to come to that person's aid. All others were to stay at their spot in case of an attack from two different directions. Dan and Joey scampered over to Bart as quickly as they could.

"I thought I heard something," Bart said excitedly.

Joey and Dan peered into the darkness and listened intently. They could hear an occasional nicker from a couple of horses.

"I think that's some of our horses that moved over your way," Joey said.

"I don't think so," Bart insisted.

"Well, I'm going to go see. Don't shoot me," Joey said and started walking into the darkness.

"Be careful. I'm telling you I heard something," Bart whispered.

Returning a couple of minutes later, Joey said, "You're lucky you didn't kill one of our horses. It was just some young geldings farting around. Don't be so jumpy."

"Jumpy? I'll show you jumpy. I'm going to the bunkhouse and jump into bed. I quit. I'll collect my pay in the morning. I signed on as a cowboy, not some darn guard," Bart said before stomping off towards the bunkhouse.

"What now?" Dan asked.

"We'll just leave Bart's spot open. I gave him the one I thought least likely to get attacked from anyways," Joey said before walking away.

Joey waited until morning light had knocked out all the shadows before rounding up the Caroline and the tired bunch of ranch hands. They walked stiffly back to the house where Claire waited on the porch to welcome them in for breakfast. As the group feasted on bacon, eggs, biscuits, and gravy, Joey told Caroline that Bart had quit and was sleeping in the bunkhouse waiting to be paid.

Waiting until she had chewed her bite of biscuit and swallowed, Caroline said, "I really can't blame him. We didn't hire Bart or anybody else for any of this. If any of you want to leave, now is the time."

The ranch hands looked from one to another to see if anybody else would quit, but with mouths full of food, each shook his head without speaking to confirm his intention to stay.

Joey and Claire also exchanged glances. Both had been surprised by Caroline's mild reaction to the news about Bart. Claire smiled ever so slightly and barely nodded her head towards Caleb as if to say that he must be the calming influence on her daughter. Joey nodded his head and made a face that conveyed that he agreed with her. Caroline never noticed the interaction between the two of them, but Caleb did. He had a pretty good idea what they were communicating and wondered if they were correct in their assessment. Also not lost on Caleb was the fact that Joey and Claire's relationship had changed significantly since Joey had been injured. He doubted his newfound sway with Caroline would hold a candle to her ire over that situation.

"A whole lot of things are going to get interesting around here," Caleb said, making a point to make eye contact with Joey and Claire.

Chapter 18

The suspense on waiting for retaliation had everyone at the Langley ranch on edge. Five days had gone by since Caleb and Caroline had killed Nathan's men. After the first night, necessity had dictated that only two people would stand guard at night. Since Joey remained limited in his physical activities, he had insisted on being one of the two. And keeping an eye on the mustang herds remained a priority. Two people from the ranch would ride out every day to cautiously to check on the horses. The journeys out to the open range had not resulted in any more encounters with ranch hands or revealed any further mischief with the mustangs. All of the extra duties had caused only the most necessary jobs on the ranch to get done while all other tasks were left to slide by the wayside.

Caroline attempted to put on a brave front as if nothing terrible had happened and continued her normally brusque ways with the ranch hands. Caleb could see that the killings were weighing heavily on her, and on more than one occasion, had caught her staring off into space as they worked.

After eating breakfast in the bunkhouse, Reese and Lucky rode out to check on the mustangs. Dan had just come in from night duty with Joey. He lay curled up in his bunk rattling the walls with his snoring. Caleb's expertise in training horses had so impressed Caroline and Joey that he now spent most of his free time working with the young horses. The shortage of help forced him to work in the corral by himself while Caroline rode out to check on the mares that had yet to be turned back loose into the wild.

Caleb stood patiently attempting to saddle his third gelding of the morning when he spied Caroline riding back in a hurry. She rode up to the corral fence and quickly slid to the ground.

"The stream that runs through the ranch is about dry this morning. It's barely running any water. I've lived here my whole life and I've never once seen it go dry. We've had plenty of rain and the snow is still melting at the higher elevations. There is no way this should be happening," Caroline said as she climbed up onto the fence.

Sitting the saddle on the ground, Caleb walked over to her. "I'm betting those booms we heard yesterday when we were out riding and couldn't figure out why it thundered on a sunny day were dynamite. Nathan has diverted the water," he said.

"That is what I've been thinking too. Thank goodness we have the pond and there are enough pools in the streambed to last a few days," she said.

"I guess they've been too busy with that to come here and bother us," he said.

"Probably. Let's go take a ride," Caroline said.

Choosing to ride Diablo, Caleb saddled the animal. The horse was still green, but no longer shied at the sight of a saddle and seemed ready to be ridden in new surroundings. Diablo had calmed significantly since his first ride and had even taken to nuzzling Caleb while being brushed.

The two of them rode out, following the stream. Traveling at an easy trot, their path weaved through the foothills as they gradually gained elevation. Caroline remained unusually quiet as they traveled. Caleb would occasionally give her a glance and see that her brow looked furrowed and her mouth remained clenched tightly shut.

Caroline caught Caleb looking at her. "More people are going to die before this is over, aren't they?" she asked.

"Probably. I think Nathan Horn would have stopped this nonsense by now if he were going to do so," Caleb replied.

"And the next time might be one of us," she said in a sad tone.

"There's always that chance," he said.

"I know this sounds silly, but when I aimed my rifle at that man, I wasn't really thinking about killing him. Things were happening so fast and I was just worried about helping you. I still have a hard time reconciling the fact that the simple act of my squeezing a trigger ended a man's life," Caroline lamented.

"Well, if you hadn't, I probably wouldn't be here right now. You have to think about what would have happened if you hadn't killed him. Life is about choices and I would hope that you would think the choice you made proved to be better than the alternative," Caleb said.

Attempting to smile, Caroline said, "I guess my answer probably changes to that question based on how annoying you are on any given day."

"I guess we're even then. There are days where you make me wish I were dead," Caleb said with a grin.

Caroline let out a giggle and slapped her thigh. "You can be witty when the mood strikes you," she said before somberness settled back over her. "Caleb, if something were to happen to you, does Joey know how to reach your family?"

Taking a big breath, Caleb sighed so loudly that Diablo perked up his ears. He slowed the horse to a walk. His heart felt as if it were trying to beat its way out of his chest. "Caroline, I need to be honest with you about my past. My real name is Berg. If you need to write my family, my father's name is Nils Berg in Chalksville,

Tennessee," he said before proceeding to recount the events back home that had led him to now be riding beside her.

Caleb had stared straight ahead as he talked, afraid to look at Caroline. As he spoke, he came to the realization that if she asked him to leave the ranch that another part of him would die just as surely as when he lost Robin. Summoning all his will power, Caleb turned his head and looked at her. Tears were streaming down her face as she looked him in the eyes. Caroline leaned over in the saddle and put her hand on his forearm, resting it there a moment. She grasped his arm and pulled him towards her. With their face inches apart, she gazed into his eyes before kissing him lightly on the lips.

As Caroline straightened herself back up in the saddle, she said, "Caleb Gunnar, you surely are a noble man. Don't ever change."

Feeling at a loss for words, Caleb looked at her blankly before turning his head and looking forward.

Caroline felt flushed and her heart raced in her chest. She didn't want to think about what she had just done or admit what the moment had meant. The walls that she had so carefully built around her were tumbling down and the notion scared the daylights out of her. She imagined using her rifle to make Joey her second victim. Not only was he becoming a suitor to her mother, but he was also the reason that Caleb came to the ranch and complicated her life in the first place. She put her heels into her horse's ribs and took off in a trot.

Spurring Diablo, Caleb kept pace with her. He felt more than pleased with his mount and preferred concentrating on the horse rather than to try to understand what had just happened with the always-unpredictable Caroline. Diablo had followed his commands and had even begun to catch on to neck reining. A covey of quail took flight and the only reaction of the gelding was to perk his ears at the burst of noise.

Caleb and Caroline passed a couple of creeks that provided what little water still flowed into the streambed. They continued on riding farther north than Caroline had ever traveled before with no sign of the blockage in sight. Both of them acted as if the kiss never happened and returned to their fallback topic of horses. As they were about to emerge from a pine grove into a clearing, Caleb held up his hand to stop. Up ahead, he spotted the newly made dam where the stream came down the mountain. A rock shelf to the left of the water had been dynamited into stream until making a barrier high enough to divert the water to run towards the southeast in the direction of Nathan Horn's ranch. Two ranch hands holding rifles stood above the dam keeping guard.

"There's your problem," Caleb said as he nodded his head toward the obstruction.

"They went to a lot of trouble to deny us water. I would have thought that killing us would have been easier than that," Caroline said sarcastically.

"I think we put a little fear into them," Caleb remarked.

"Surely not enough. I'm afraid we are defeated and they have won," she said with resignation.

"Not necessarily. I know you think us southern boys are slower than molasses on a frosty day, but I've helped blow up a bridge or two in my day during the war," Caleb bragged.

"Slow talking, yes, but I certainly never thought that you were slow of mind. How much dynamite would it take to open that back?" Caroline asked.

"It would probably take a few sticks, but all we really need to do is weaken the dam enough that the water will do the rest. Do you have any dynamite at the ranch?" he asked.

"I don't know. I know Joey uses it to blow out stumps, but I have no idea if he has any on hand. Won't it take a long fuse not to blow yourself to pieces?" she asked.

"Long enough," Caleb replied with a grin. "I think I have a plan. Let's get back to the ranch."

By the time Caleb and Caroline returned to the ranch, the sun sat low to the west. They put their horses up for the night and brushed them down while the animals munched on oats.

As they walked out of the barn, Caroline said, "Why don't you have dinner with us tonight. That way you can talk with Joey because I'm sure Mother has found a reason that he needs to stay in the house for one more night."

"Caroline, I want to ask you a question. Has your mother been happier since Joey has been staying with you?" Caleb asked.

Narrowing her eyes, Caroline gave Caleb a frosty look. "Yes, she has," she said reluctantly.

"That's something to think about - at least it is if you care about her happiness," he said as they walked towards the house.

In a playful voice instead of her usual annoyed tone, Caroline said, "I must have hired you for your opinions instead of ranch work because I believe I get a whole lot more of them than I do actual labor."

Inside the home, they found Joey sitting at the kitchen table watching Claire prepare supper. Both looked towards the entrance of the kitchen with surprised expressions on their faces at seeing Caleb with Caroline.

"Caleb will be dining with us this evening. He needs to discuss some things with Joey. I'm going to my room to clean up before dinner," Caroline said before whisking out of the kitchen.

"You can wash up in here, Caleb. You won't be in my way," Claire said as she rolled chicken in flour.

By the time that Claire finished forking the fried chicken out of the skillet and onto a china platter, Caroline returned from her room. She walked into the kitchen wearing a store bought red calico dress, fitted at the waist, and sporting white lace on the sleeve ends and around the neck. Her naturally wavy hair hung loosely on her shoulders. Claire had her back to her daughter and did not see the entrance, but Caleb and Joey certainly did. Caleb had never witnessed Caroline in anything but men's clothing with her hair pinned so tightly to her head that she looked boyish. He did a double take at the unexpected sight. Caroline looked prettier than he had even imagined and her attractiveness sent an ache shooting through his body that reminded him how long he had been alone.

Claire turned to set the platter of chicken on the table and spied her daughter. "Oh, my, what's the occasion?" she asked without thinking.

Taken aback by her mother's inquiry, Caroline said, "No occasion. Even I like to dress up once in a while."

Standing, Caleb pulled out a chair for Caroline. "I think you look nice. I never realized that you were a girl until now," he joked as he helped her scoot up to the table.

Joey and Claire exchanged glances, their eyes betraying merriment at the sudden change in demeanor between Caleb and Caroline.

After the food had been passed around the table, Joey asked, "So what is the big news?"

"I noticed that out stream looked nearly dry this morning. Caleb and I rode clear up to where Nathan's men have dammed the water. Caleb can tell you his plan," Caroline said.

Caleb paused to let Caroline's succinct delivery have time to register with Joey and Claire. "They have two men guarding the dam. We're going to need some dynamite and a long fuse. They can see us coming forever so we'll have to blow the dam up at night. I figure that we should get there before dark to get the lay of the land. Dan and Reese can get above them and distract them with gunfire. I'll sneak in, plant the dynamite, and run the fuse. They'll be too busy to notice me or see the fuse lit," he said.

Joey set his fork down and ran his hand through his hair. "I can't understand what's gotten into Nathan. I'm going with you. I trust Dan, but I have my doubts about Reese and Lucky when things get rough and I'm not about to let you get killed because of them," Joey said.

"You are in no condition to be on horseback," Claire said.

"I can ride. It's about time I started working around here again. The men are going to lose respect for me I don't. I'll be fine," Joey assured Claire.

"It's a long ride to the dam," Caleb warned.

"Trust me, I'm ready to ride," Joey said.

"Do you have any dynamite?" Caleb asked.

"I did when I left in the fall. I'll check in the morning. I know I had nearly a full spool of fuse," Joey replied.

"Caleb, are you sure you can do this without getting yourself killed?" Claire asked.

"Ma'am, I've worked with dynamite a fair amount on the farm in my time. I'll be fine. I didn't ride all the way out west just to blow myself to pieces. We'll be ready to celebrate late tomorrow night," Caleb answered.

"I'm going too," Caroline chimed in.

"I think that Joey, Dan, and I will about have things covered," Caleb reasoned.

"I don't care what you have covered. I'm not going to sit around here all day and wonder if the three of you have blown yourselves to bits. I'm going," Caroline stated.

Picking up the platter, Claire offered Caleb more chicken after she noticed the young man had devoured a leg. "I guess things are settled. Let's talk of happier things. Caleb, tell us a little about your family," she said.

Caleb proceeded to tell of his former life, leaving out the name of his hometown or any of the events concerning Charles. Neither Joey nor Caroline had bothered to tell Claire that Caleb had lost his wife and baby. The news made her emotional. She swiped a tear away as she listened of Caleb's past and offered her condolences.

Afterwards, Claire changed the subject to tales of Caroline's childhood. She took considerable pleasure in telling of the time that a fox had killed one of their chickens and Caroline had snuck the orphaned eggs into her bed to keep them warm, only to wake in the morning covered in yolks. The image of a young Caroline covered in egg made Caleb laugh so hard that he snorted and Joey smacked the table in his amusement.

Caleb stood after everyone had finished eating. "I best be getting back to the bunkhouse. Thank you for a good meal. It certainly tasted better than what I would have had," he said.

"I will join you," Joey said. "I need to move back there myself."

"You can stay one more night," Claire insisted. "I'm checking those ribs in the morning before we decide if you're capable of riding. Step out back with me so that we can see what the weather is doing."

Claire whisked Joey away, leaving Caleb with Caroline.

Realizing what Claire had done for him, Caleb stood there awkwardly trying to think of something to say now that he had crossed into unfamiliar territory with Caroline. "I was just teasing you earlier. You really do look beautiful," he finally said.

Caroline's forward nature seemed to have vanished with her men's clothing. She appeared embarrassed by the compliment and unsure of herself. If somebody had been watching, they would have sworn that they were viewing two thirteen years old making their first awkward attempt at courting.

"Thank you," she said quietly.

Caleb wanted to curse himself aloud for feeling so helpless. Considering that he had once been bold with the girls, he now felt as unsure of himself as a foal taking its first step. He knew that he wanted to kiss Caroline, but the thought of it made his pulse quicken with anxiety. Wanting desperately not to regret this moment, he bent down, slowly moving his head towards hers. He leaned in and kissed her. Their lips lingered longer than he had planned and he kissed her again more fervently. To his surprise, Caleb found Caroline willing. He became lost in the kiss until breaking it off abruptly when he feared embarrassing himself if the moment lasted any longer.

"I guess I better get to the bunkhouse. Goodnight, Caroline," he said as he straightened his posture.

"Goodnight, Caleb. I'll see you in the morning," Caroline said before standing and giving Caleb one more quick kiss.

Chapter 19

While eating breakfast, Claire held court in a positively bubbly mood. Caroline watched her mother, wondering the reason for such perky behavior considering the magnitude of what lay ahead for the day. She herself felt tired and grumpy after having slept fitfully during night while worrying about blowing up the dam.

Joey gobbled his breakfast down and excused himself. He left the house anxious to go check on his stash of dynamite.

"I got me a little sugar last night out on the back porch. How about you?" Claire said with a grin.

"Mother, please," Caroline whined.

"Oh, quit being such a prude. I'm just letting you know that Joey and I are very fond of each other. If you love me, you should be pleased that I've found happiness again. After your daddy died, I sure did not think that possible," Claire said.

"I do want to see you happy. I really thought that you and I were past having men in our lives and I just need some time to get used to the idea that somebody might be replacing Daddy," Caroline replied.

"Nobody could ever replace your daddy. We were together far too long and worked too hard side by side for that to be so, but Joey does make me feel like I'm more than just a relic from the past," Claire said.

"Okay. I understand and I'll try to do better," Caroline said meekly.

"Now, what about you? Don't tell me that you decided to wear a dress last night just on a whim. What's going on?" Claire inquired.

Caroline tried to give her mother a stern "mind your own business" look, but failed, breaking into a smile. "I might have gotten a little sugar last night too," she said.

Popping the table with her hand, Claire said, "I knew it. I could feel something in the air as soon as you two walked in yesterday evening. Caleb is a fine young man."

"He grows on you, I'll give him that," Caroline said begrudgingly.

"I'm proud of you for peeking over that wall you've built around yourself," her mother said.

"Don't make so much out of it. I might come to my senses tomorrow. Caleb is just a man and human nature probably just got the better of me," Caroline said.

Claire let out a loud giggle. "Oh, you're funny. You wanted human nature to get the best of you. I'd be careful if I were you. That's where babies come from," Claire said with a laugh.

"I have to get to work, but I can assure you that I still have a fortress around the spot where babies come from," Caroline said as she stood and headed out of the kitchen. She could still hear her mother giggling as she walked out the front door.

Caroline found all the ranch hands still inside the bunkhouse. Joey and Caleb stood in the corner next to an old wardrobe that the cowboys used to store things. Caleb looked preoccupied studying the dynamite that he held in his hands.

"How do things look?" Caroline asked as she approached the two men.

"We're in good shape. There's more than enough dynamite and the sticks still look fresh. We were thinking that we could get some things done around here this morning and then leave sometime after lunch," Caleb said.

"That sounds good to me. We have to get these horses trained. Have you told Dan?" Caroline said.

"He knows," Joey informed her.

Caleb and Dan spent the rest of the morning breaking young horses while Lucky and Reese worked with the green broke ones. Joey decided to see how he held up on a horse and rode with Caroline to check on the pastured animals. He found the riding uncomfortable but nothing that he didn't think he could handle. The group met back at the bunkhouse at noon. Caroline headed to the house to have lunch with her mother, but Joey made a point of staying with the other cowboys to eat with them. He did his best to lighten the somber mood of the ranch hands by telling some of his well-worn jokes.

After eating, the ranch hands spent another couple of hours working the horses as Caroline and Joey watched on. Joey eventually walked to the bunkhouse to retrieve the dynamite, caps, and fuse. By the time he had his saddlebags packed, the others joined him with their horses. The group rode out, leaving Reese and Lucky with instructions to stay close to the house and keep a close eye out for any unwelcome visitors.

The riding wore on Joey after a couple of hours. Every breath sent a shooting pain through his chest until he had to stop and rest for a quarter of an hour. Caroline tried to talk him into heading home, but Joey would not hear of it. Once he recovered, they resumed their travel and made the rest of the trip without another stop. The sun sat just above the western horizon as they reached the pine grove. They tied the horses in the middle of the trees and walked to the edge to have a look. In the distance, two men could still be seen standing guard over the dam.

"Are you sure we have enough dynamite?" Joey asked upon seeing the dam.

"Sure, with all that water pressure against it, that dam will give way once the dynamite weakens the center," Caleb assured him.

"Looks like Dan and I can make our way up either side of the streambed and go around those two guards to get above them. One of us will have to wade the new stream. Up above there's rock on one side and trees on the other for cover," Joey noted.

"Are you sure that you can walk that far?" Caroline asked.

"I'll be fine. I'm more worried about walking back if we don't kill those two," Joey replied.

"After the explosion, they won't know up from down," Caleb assured him.

"I guess it's settled them. I'm going to take a nap. Wake me when it's time," Joey said before finding a spot thick with pine needles and bedding down.

Night settled over the land as Joey snored softly under the pines. The new moon made things so dark that the group could barely see each other and only the guards' campfire colored the pitch black surrounding.

Caleb shook Joey. "It's time to get busy," he said.

"Good. I'm getting too old for this sleeping on the ground," Joey said as he stood and worked the kinks out of his back.

"I'll wade the stream. You might slip and bust another rib," Dan said.

"On another day, I might be insulted, but tonight I'll take dry feet and keep my mouth shut. I'll give you a whistle when I'm in position. You should be ready long before me at the pace I travel these days," Joey said.

"Let's go then," Dan said.

As Joey and Dan's footsteps faded into the darkness, Caleb retrieved the explosives from Joey's saddlebag.

"Are you sure that you can see well enough to do this?" Caroline asked.

"I already picked my spot out and I think I can find it. I'll just shove the cap in, plant the dynamite, and then run the fuse," Caleb said.

"What about when it explodes?" she asked.

"I have that figured out too. Don't worry. I'll be fine. Make sure you cover your ears when you see the sparks from the fuse. We're going to be making some noise," he said in a voice brimming with confidence in order to calm Caroline's worries.

"I'll be glad when we are headed home," Caroline said.

"We will be soon. I'm going to start walking that way. Just sit tight and don't worry," Caleb said. He longed to give her a hug and a kiss, but thought that now was not the time. The image of hugging the mercurial Caroline with explosives in his hands ran through his mind and he smiled in the dark at the irony.

Caroline reached out and patted his arm. "Be careful," she said.

Caleb set out towards the dam, heading straight up the now dry riverbed. He walked what he guessed to be two-thirds of the way based on the guards' campfire and stopped. Time seemed to be passing at a snail's pace as Caleb waited for Joey and Dan to begin the distraction.

By the time Joey made his way around the guards, his chest felt as if a knife were piercing it and he struggled to catch his breath. Even in the cool night air, his face was beaded with sweat and he had to use his sleeve to wipe out his eyes. He took a position behind some rocks and peeked over at the guards below him. The two men were sitting in the shadows well away from the fire. As Joey raised his rifle, he found that he couldn't even see his sights when he aimed at the guards. He cursed for not bringing shotguns and attempting to sneak close enough to their camp to blast them. Letting out a whistle, Joey pointed his rifle at the fire to see his sights and then aimed his gun towards a guard.

Caleb nearly jumped out of his skin when the crack of a rifle shattered the silence. As the exchange of gunfire erupted, he resumed his march. He reached the dam and stared at the rocks until his eyes could make out their shapes. The guards were probably no farther than forty feet away and the roar of their rifles made concentrating an effort.

The only time Joey had any idea where the guards were hiding was when he saw the fire explode out of their gun barrels. He wasn't too fond of the idea of keeping his head up to watch in case one of the fools got lucky with a shot and he lost his bearing the moment things went black again anyways. Dan followed his lead and they alternated taking turns shooting their rifles just enough to keep the guards preoccupied.

By the time Caleb located the spot he wanted to plant the dynamite, the gun fighting had slowed into occasional shots. Working rapidly, he attached the fuse to the blasting cap and shoved it into one of the sticks of dynamite before working the sticks in between two large rocks. He began walking back down the side of the streambed, unwinding the whole roll of fuse as he went until he reached the end of it. Some boulder to the side of the bed would provide him some cover from the blast. After lighting the fuse, Caleb hustled behind the rock and covered his ears. He peeked out to watch the fuse burn towards the dam and squatted back down just before the explosion. The noise still felt deafening even with his ears covered and the percussion knocked him on his butt. A shower of gravel rained down on him. As Caleb stood, he could hear the pent-up water come barreling back down the streambed. He smiled with the knowledge that his mission was accomplished and set out for the pine grove.

Joey stuck his little fingers in his ears and shook them. The noise from the explosion had been louder than he expected and his ears were ringing. He looked down towards the campfire. A cloud of dust and gravel nearly obscured its light. He wondered if the explosion had killed the guards, but had no plans to stick around to find out and headed back.

Caleb reached the pine grove. "Caroline, it's me," he called out.

"I'm over here. Are you okay?" Caroline asked.

"I'm fine," he replied.

"I could hear the water coming," she said excitedly.

"Yeah, it worked. Let's hope we hear Joey and Dan coming next," Caleb said.

Dan returned first after a wait that seemed to go on forever. Joey arrived a good ten minutes later. Both men were unharmed.

"So did you hit either one of them?" Caleb asked.

"I don't think so. Our first shots were the only ones that really had a chance and even then they were sitting back away from the fire far enough that drawing a bead on them proved nearly impossible," Joey said.

"I don't know what happened to them after the explosion. I kept an eye out as I walked back but they didn't go near their fire if they were still alive," Dan added.

"It doesn't matter. Caleb accomplished what we set out to do. I'm ready to go home," Joey said.

The ride home in the moonless night was slow going. Caroline, relieved that the dam was destroyed and that nobody got hurt, became reflective as weariness set in. She began reminiscing about her father and all his dreams and plans for the ranch. Dan had never witnessed Caroline in such an unguarded and nostalgic state. Joey smiled in the dark as he listened to her talk. He wondered how big of a part Caleb coming into her life played in her vulnerable behavior. Caroline sounded like the person that he remembered before her husband ran off and the death of Jackson Langley.

By the time they reached the ranch, it was nearly two in the morning. Joey lit the oil lamps in the barn and the exhausted crew unsaddled their horses and put them in stalls.

Once all the animals were fed, Caroline faced the ranch hands. In an emotional and weary voice, she said, "Gentlemen, I want to thank you for what you did for us tonight. I know that none of you signed up for this kind of thing and could all leave for a safer job. I am truly beholden to each of you."

Chapter 20

Claire had cajoled Joey into a promise to take her to church on Sunday morning, but after he and the others didn't make it back to the ranch until nearly two in the morning the previous night, she decided to let him sleep. She had heard Caroline come in and had gotten up to check on her daughter. Caroline was hungry and Claire fixed her some eggs and bacon while insisting on hearing about the evening's undertaking. By the time the food was cooked, Caroline could barely stay awake to eat it. Claire went back to bed and slept like a baby after learning that the night had been a success and that all were safe.

Reese and Lucky were up doing chores and Claire got them to hitch her buggy. She headed out for the church over the mild objections of her ranch hands for her safety. Most Sundays she went by herself anyways on the five-mile trek to the church. She always liked making the journey and got to enjoy the view of the mountains. As she pulled the buggy into the churchyard, she spied Nathan and Milo Horn, Thomas Rhodes, and a couple other ranchers smoking under a tree. Nathan saw her and began walking towards the buggy as Claire climbed out of the rig.

"Are things a little dry on the ranch?" Nathan asked with a smirk.

"Nathan, we have known each other a long time. Why are you doing this?" Claire asked.

"This is a hard land and only the strong and mighty prosper. All the rest get squished like bugs. That's what I am to do. When I am done, that daughter of yours is going to wish she had stayed in the kitchen where she belongs.

She should have married Milo if she wanted to be part of a successful ranch," he said.

"Is that what this is about? Do you resent a woman running a ranch?" Claire asked.

Avoiding the questions, Nathan said, "Your bunch already killed two of my men."

"I don't think they had much choice in the matter. We're standing in front of a church. Do you think what you are doing is godly?" Claire demanded.

"For all you know, God just might be on my side. It's about time for church to start," he said.

"By the way, our stream was running just fine this morning. I believe one of God's angels may have smitten your dam last night," Claire said.

"What?" Nathan yelled. His face turned red with anger and the veins in his temples bulged as he grew visibly flustered.

Claire watched as Nathan stormed off towards Milo, grabbing his son by the arm, and leading him towards their buggy. The two men climbed in and then Nathan laid the whip to his horse, taking off with a lurch. Claire watched the carriage disappear down the road before walking into the church and taking her regular seat. She could feel some of the members staring at her and the thought of them wondering how mild little Claire had run off big, bad Nathan, made her smile.

After the sermon, Claire spent a few minutes talking to the wives of some the ranchers. Without mentioning anyone by name, she made a point of informing the women that the ranch was having problems with someone trying to ruin their livelihood. She knew that her confrontation with Nathan would spread from ranch to ranch and she wanted to make sure that the other ranchers knew that the Langley ranch was the victim and not the aggressor. Satisfied that she had won over her fellow ranch wives, Claire left for home.

As Claire returned to the ranch, she saw Caroline and all the men standing around a fire in the spot that they occasionally used for a cooking pit. She couldn't imagine what was going on and drove the buggy right up to the crowd to find out for herself. Reese had gone hunting after the morning chores and killed a turkey. By the time he returned home, everyone from the late night expedition had arisen, and upon seeing the bird, Caroline had suggested a cookout. The ranch hands had jumped at the suggestion and the turkey now roasted over the flame.

Claire smiled at her daughter to try to conceal the wave of emotion that was about to get the best of her. A month ago, Caroline would have turned brusque at the mere suggestion of such frivolity and insisted on at least a half days work from the crew. Somehow, someway, Caleb was helping her daughter find the person she had been before life had gotten so hard. Claire suppressed the urge to climb out of the buggy to give him a big hug.

"I'll unhitch your buggy for you," Caleb volunteered.

"Why, thank you. Climb in with me," Claire suggested.

The two headed towards the shed where they stored the carriage.

As Claire watched Caleb work, she said, "Caleb, I don't know what magic you are working on Caroline, but keep up the good work. She's acted more like her old self in the last week than the whole last two years."

"Ma'am, I don't think I've worked any magic with her unless making her mad counts," Caleb said with a laugh.

"I think you've done more than that," she said.

Caleb looked over at Claire. Her smile made him feel awkward. He wasn't sure if she was hinting at knowing more than she was telling and he stammered for a moment. "We do seem to be getting along better," he finally offered.

"You must be doing something right to get her into a dress. I'm not trying to pry, but I did want to thank you for being so good to Caroline. I admit she's a handful, but I can't help but believe she's worth it," Claire said.

"Yes, ma'am," Caleb said as he led the horse away towards the barn.

Claire walked to the house to change clothes and start preparing side dishes. Caroline joined her and began helping with the cooking.

"You don't care that I suggested the cookout, do you?" Caroline asked.

"For Heaven's sake, no. Everybody has been stressed and working through the night. They deserve a day to relax," Claire replied.

"What did you and Caleb talk about?" Caroline inquired.

"Nothing much. He's not a big talker," Claire answered.

"Mother," Caroline said skeptically.

"I did thank him for looking out for you with all that's been going on around here," Claire said.

Narrowing her eyes, Caroline peered at her mother, but got no further response from her so she dropped the subject.

As they peeled potatoes, Claire told Caroline about her encounter with Nathan Horn.

"I'm proud of you," Caroline said when her mother finished talking.

"I just had enough of his blustery ways. I made sure to let the other ranch wives know what was going on too. No need for them to think we wanted any part of this nonsense," Claire said as she pumped some water into a pan.

Once they finished cooking the mashed potatoes, gravy, corn, and peas, Claire and Caroline brought the food out and set it upon the old picnic table that Jackson Langley had made years ago. The turkey had finished roasting and Caleb and Dan carried it over and placed it on a platter. Everyone crowded around the table and Claire handed Joey a carving knife, asking him to do the honors. The symbolism wasn't lost on Caroline as she watched Joey go to work on the bird.

Seeing Caroline in such a carefree and chatty mood put the others more at ease than usual around their boss. The ranch hands laughed and told stories throughout the meal. Claire and Caroline contributed to the conversations and giggled along with their employees. When Claire wasn't exchanging glances with Joey, she observed Caleb and Caroline watching each other. The two weren't exactly flirting, but they were certainly very enthralled with each other. Caleb told of a trip to Illinois where a waitress had told him she loved to hear him talk but that by the time he got to the end of a sentence she had forgotten the beginning of it. The group broke into laughter and Caroline giggled so hard that an unladylike snort escaped her.

As the meal was coming to an end, Caroline said, "Dan, why don't you go get your fiddle. I feel like dancing."

Dan looked befuddled by the request of his boss. He appeared to have spied a devil growing wings and a halo right before his eyes. "Oh, sure," he said before scampering towards the bunkhouse.

The ranch hand quickly returned with his instrument. Dan played barn dances with other musicians and had a reputation for having a fine voice and playing a lively fiddle. He led off with "Old Dan Tucker". Caroline took Caleb's hand and began dancing. Claire did the same with Joey though he didn't really dance with his injury, but did move his feet a little and let Claire twirl on his hand. No sooner had the song ended than Dan started in on "Buffalo

Gals". Lucky and Reese seemed reluctant to ask their employers for a turn, but the two ladies went to them and tugged on their hands. Dan, sensing the changing fortunes of Caleb and Joey with the two women of the ranch, chose "Kiss Waltz" for his next piece. Caleb and Caroline began waltzing. Caroline made a point of keeping her eyes gazing directly into Caleb's as they danced. Her boldness made him feel shy and he had to fight his instincts not to look away. He gave her his best smile to hide his feelings. Joey made a valiant if somewhat stiff attempt at the dance as he and Claire waltzed on the grass.

As Dan drew the bow across the strings for the last notes of the song, Joey noticed two riders approaching. Caleb reached down, removing the thong from the hammer of his Colt and stepped to the side to have an unhindered view of the men. Nathan Horn and Frankie Myers rode up to the group. Frankie still had his broken hand in a splint and looked as ornery as ever.

"I didn't mean to break up the party," Nathan said.

"What do you want, Nathan?" Claire asked.

"Your boys sure snuffed the fight out of my two men. They look like they got blasted with rock salt. They have cuts and bruises from head to toe and they're about deaf. Poor old Eddie was just getting over the licking your man gave him in the saloon," Nathan said.

"Did you ride all the way over here to tell us that?" Claire demanded.

"No, I came to see if we could come to a truce. I can't afford to lose any more men and I was hoping we could forget that all this ever happened," Nathan said.

"So you've changed your mind since this morning about squishing us like bugs and putting Caroline in the kitchen where she belongs?" Claire asked.

Caroline took a step forward. "We would love to see all the shenanigans come to a stop. I'm not sure that truce is the right word since we were only protecting what is ours and were never the aggressor," she said.

"Well, let's just say that we all agree to leave each other alone and go about our own business then. This ranch has proved my equal and I certainly didn't squish anyone," Nathan said.

"That sounds good," Caroline said.

Caleb stepped towards Frankie's horse. "What about you? Are you willing to let bygones be bygones?" Caleb asked as he looked up at the ranch hand.

Frankie looked over at his boss and Nathan gave a small nod of his head. "Sure, I do what Mr. Horn wants. He pays my salary. I'm not much use anyways and will probably have to learn how to shoot left-handed seeing how you about ruined my right hand," he said.

"I'd probably be dead if I hadn't," Caleb said.

Nathan held up his hand and waved it. "Okay, enough of this. I got what I came for and we best be on our way. Good day," he said before turning his horse and riding off with Frankie following him.

After the two men had ridden out of sight, Claire said, "I wonder what that was all about."

"I'm guessing that Nathan is trying to get us to let our guard down and give himself some time to lick his wounds. He doesn't strike me as the type to give up that easily," Joey said.

"That's what I was thinking," Caleb added.

"I embarrassed him at church today and I suspect that Nathan has a long memory," Claire noted.

"We better keep up our watch over the herds and at night around here," Joey said.

As Caroline turned towards Dan, she said, "Dan, do you still have some music left in you? Let's have one afternoon without worrying about Nathan. I was just starting to get warmed up good."

Chapter 21

Nearly a week had gone by with no signs of trouble from Nathan Horn or his men. The tension that had gripped the Langley ranch began to ease. A considerable amount of time and energy still went into keeping a night watch and daily checks on the mustang herds, but the crew had adjusted to the schedule and weren't as nervous in their travels.

Caleb and Caroline had an uneventful week and that's what had Caleb confused. After seeing the bold and carefree side of Caroline dancing away the previous Sunday, she had given him no clues on how she felt towards him since then. Caroline had resumed her obsession with every detail concerning the ranch, albeit in a much kinder way. Even Lucky had commented over dinner one night about Caroline's change in tone when issuing orders. Caleb had no idea whether Caroline had second thoughts about the turn in their relationship or whether she planned to wait for him to take the next step. He had even contemplated trying to have a word with Claire concerning her daughter, but lost his nerve when the opportunity presented itself. The realization that he had become so awkward towards women made him feel disgusted with himself. There had been a time when he wouldn't have thought twice about letting a girl know his intentions, but that was before life kicked the snot out of him.

After eating supper on Saturday night, Caleb headed to the barn. He felt as if he had been neglecting Leif with all that had been going on and planned to take the horse for a ride. As he walked inside the barn, he was surprised to see Caroline brushing down Buddy. He hadn't seen her since that morning when she left with Joey to check on the mustangs and he had stayed to work the horses.

"I wasn't expecting to see you in here," Caleb said.

"I needed to give Buddy a good brushing and wanted to check his feet," Caroline said as she lifted the horse's front leg.

Caleb watched her work, a little taken aback that she hadn't bothered to stop what she was doing to talk to him. He stood there waiting on her until the silence caught her attention and she put the horses foot down and turned towards him. For a moment, he contemplated telling Caroline to have a nice evening and walking over to Leif's stall. He chided himself for his cowardice inclinations and decided that rejection had to be better than the uncertainty.

"I was wondering if we might go on a picnic tomorrow or something," he said.

Caroline smiled. "I was wondering if my kissing wasn't up to your southern standards - or something. So are you asking me out on a picnic?" she said teasingly.

Grinning, Caleb said, "Well, you are the boss. I thought maybe you had to be in charge of everything, but yes, I am asking you."

"Well, maybe I'm an old fashioned girl when it comes to some things. Are you fixing the food?" Caroline asked.

"I will as long as you don't complain about the taste," he said.

"I better do it then. No need for a bellyache on a pretty day. We're liable to run out of chickens around here with the way you gnaw on legs and thighs," she said.

Inhaling deeply and letting out a sigh, Caleb felt the tension vanish from his muscles. Hearing Caroline's banter and knowing that she had been waiting on him to take the lead had relaxed him. He realized that he was getting ahead of himself in his feelings for her, but he couldn't help it. Being in Caroline's company made him feel hopeful that life might be finally ready to get better.

"Maybe I should check that you still meet my southern standards before we waste a perfectly fine Sunday," Caleb teased.

"I wouldn't waste a lot of time talking if I were you. A girl could get out of the mood waiting for you to finish a sentence," Caroline countered.

Stepping forward, Caleb wrapped his arms around Caroline. He felt emboldened by their conversation and kissed her hard on the mouth. She wrapped her arms around him as their mouths locked together. The couple was lost in the moment and didn't hear the footsteps until it proved too late.

"You two better be careful. I hear that stuff is as addictive as laudanum," Joey teased as he walked into the barn.

Caleb spun around and stood next to Caroline, looking like two kids caught stealing candy from a store.

In an annoyed voice, Caleb asked, "What are you doing in here?"

"I was going to replace a tie string on my saddle. The leather is about shot. I didn't know I wasn't allowed in the barn. Maybe you should hang a bell above the door," Joey said, grinning like a Cheshire cat.

"I'm taking Leif for a ride," Caleb said before walking towards the horse's stall.

"You better not tell Mother. I don't want her asking me fifty questions," Caroline warned Joey.

Joey stood there smiling at Caroline. "I won't say a thing, but when even poor old Lucky has figured things out, I'm not sure there's much left to hide. You two are adults after all - though sometimes I have to remind myself that it is so," he said before walking past her towards the tack room.

Caroline resumed checking her horse's feet while Caleb saddled Leif. He led the horse out of the stall as she finished her inspection.

"I guess I'll see you tomorrow," Caleb said.

Walking over to Caleb, Caroline gave him a big smacker on the lips. "You should have left that old codger on the side of the road," she said.

"I wouldn't be here now if I had done that," he said.

"I wasn't looking for logic. I wanted a little commiserating," she said with a grin.

"Okay, I'll commiserate with you all you want tomorrow," Caleb promised.

Caroline burst into a giggle and turned red with embarrassment for the things that flashed through her mind at Caleb's remark.

∞

On Sunday morning, Joey awakened the other four ranch hands while getting ready for church with his humming while he shaved.

"Getting ready plenty early, don't you think?" Caleb hollered.

"I woke up early thinking about what all the church ladies will be saying after seeing Claire and me there together," Joey answered.

"Unless you got something to be ashamed of, I wouldn't care what they thought," Caleb mumbled in his sleepy state.

"I certainly have nothing to be ashamed of, and you are right, it doesn't matter. Go back to sleep," Joey said.

By the time that Joey started banging pans while cooking his breakfast, the others gave up on sleep and crawled out of their bunks. Dan badgered Joey until the foreman agreed to cook breakfast for the whole crew since they were up anyways.

After the crew finished eating, Joey gave his boots a quick brush over before heading out to get the buggy ready. He retrieved the horse and had it hitched to the rig just in time to get Claire. Driving to the front of the house, he sauntered up the steps and knocked on the door. Claire let him into the home.

"Let me go get my bonnet and I'll be ready," Claire said before scurrying off towards her bedroom.

The smell of frying chicken permeated the house. Joey peeked his head into the kitchen and saw Caroline standing over the stove.

"I hear there's going to be a picnic today," Joey said.

Caroline jumped at the sound of a voice and turned her head to look over her shoulder at Joey. "I hear there is going to be a dinner in town," she countered.

"Remember what I told you about those addictions," he teased.

Shaking her tongs at him, Caroline said, "Joey Clemson, you don't want to get on my bad side."

"I'm ready," Claire announced.

With a grin, Joey gave Caroline a wink before leading Claire to the buggy and helping her into it. They rode away towards the church. Claire looked forward to seeing the reactions of the other women to her bringing Joey with her. She felt brazen and a little nervous and chatted the entire trip to calm her nerves.

As they rode into the churchyard, Claire spotted a group of women standing outside talking. Nelly Nixon saw Claire too and must have said something because the rest of the ladies turned their heads much too quickly to look even slightly subtle. Claire grinned and waved at them before Joey helped her down from the carriage.

When church started, Preacher Hobbs made a big to do about their visitor and made Joey stand up and introduce himself. Joey turned red, but stood and did as the preacher asked. Claire loved the attention. She'd been labeled the poor ranch widow with the impetuous daughter long enough and wanted to be seen as something more.

Joey listened to the sermon attentively and worked up the nerve to hold Claire's hand. Once the service finished, Preacher Hobbs thanked Joey for coming and invited him back next Sunday. Several church members came up to Joey and welcomed him. Nathan and Milo Horn made a show of walking over and speaking to Joey and Claire for a moment as the couple climbed into the buggy.

On the ride to town, the two of them discussed the sermon and Nathan's apparent change of heart towards ruining the ranch. An uncomfortable silence fell upon them and they rode a mile without talking.

Claire finally turned to Joey. "You know I love to dance, but I'm getting tired of leading," she said.

With a confused expression, Joey took a moment to realize that Claire had spoken metaphorically.

"You are, are you?" he said with a smile. "I don't have much experience leading after a life lived as a ranch hand."

"You are the foreman," Claire reminded him.

Letting out a laugh, Joey said, "Well, how about we go ahead and just come out and tell everybody that we are a courting. I can start spending more time with you that way and not feel as if I'm sneaking around like a kid."

"That sounds like a good beginning to me. If I were you, I wouldn't move to slow though. A lonely old widow might not be in the mood to wait on her beau forever. That bed starts getting cold around the fall," she said.

Joey turned red for the second time that day. "Yes, ma'am, I'll surely keep that in mind," he said.

Claire let out a giggle and slapped Joey on the leg before changing the subject. "Thank goodness Caleb asked Caroline on a picnic today. She never said anything but I could tell that this week wasn't going to her satisfaction," she said.

"I wouldn't worry about those two. That bud is about ready to bloom," Joey said.

∞

Caleb worked at hitching the team of horses to the buckboard. By the time he set his Winchester rifle in the back of the wagon, Caroline had joined him carrying the picnic basket, a blanket, and her rifle. She wore a blue dress and stood there smiling and feeling shy in her feminine attire.

As Caleb took the gun and basket from her, he said, "You look pretty today. As we say back home, you clean up real good."

"Thank you. I don't know what it says about me anymore when I feel more comfortable in men's clothing than I do a dress," Caroline said.

"You just haven't had the opportunity to get reacquainted with that side of you in a good long while," Caleb said as he helped her up onto the seat of the wagon. He climbed up beside her. "Where are we headed?"

"Do you remember that grassy knoll along the stream about a mile from here? It has nice shade. I've always thought that it's a pretty spot."

"I do," he said as he popped the reins against the horses' rumps to get them moving.

Neither Caleb nor Caroline seemed to know what to talk about as they followed the streambed in the wagon.

With all that both of them had been through in their lives, each started having second thoughts about what they were getting themselves into now that they were actually on a date.

Caleb rubbed his chin. To end the silence, he said, "I wore a long beard for years until I headed out here. It still feels odd to touch my face. I kept my hair cut neat too."

"I don't like beards. They are for men that need to hide the ugly," Caroline said with a laugh. "Your hair is too pretty to keep short."

"I guess I'll take that as a compliment. I'm not sure being pretty is what I'm after though," he said.

Caroline playfully tapped his shoulder with her hand. "I'm sure Frankie Myers doesn't think you are pretty, but it's all right if I do," she said.

"If you say so," he said.

"Can you believe that I was one of those girls that liked to play with my dolls all the time and had no interest in horses?" Caroline asked.

Looking over at her, Caleb smiled. "No, I cannot. That must have been ages ago," he teased.

"I'm not that old," she replied.

Once they reached the knoll, Caleb helped Caroline from the wagon before retrieving the basket and guns. She spread the blanket on the ground and pulled out the food and dishes from the basket. Caleb walked back to the wagon and retrieved a bottle of wine wrapped in a towel that he'd stashed under the seat.

"Where did you get that?" Caroline asked in surprise as he removed the bottle from its wrapping.

"Joey gave it to me. He said he had a couple of them that he'd been saving for a special occasion and wanted us to have one," Caleb said.

"Really? That was sweet. He's just full of surprises," she said.

"He probably just felt guilty for catching us last night and trying his best to embarrass us," he said.

"I think it has more to do with just being nice. I think he enjoyed every minute of teasing us," Caroline said as she looked into the basket. "I forgot cups."

"Joey didn't give me anything to use to open the bottle," Caleb said as he pulled his penknife from his pocket and began digging out the cork. He worked at it a couple of minutes before getting the stopper out mainly in one piece. "A little cork never hurt anyone."

Caleb passed the bottle to Caroline and she tipped it up and took a swallow.

"I haven't had wine in so long that I about forgot what it tastes like. That's pretty good," she said and passed the bottle back.

After taking a sip, Caleb puckered his face. "It's sweet. I might need a sip or two to get used to it," he said.

The couple started in eating the chicken, baked beans, and corn. As they passed the bottle back and forth, the wine began to relax them and they commenced joking around and giggling. By the time that Caleb cleaned the meat from the bone of his second chicken leg, the couple had lost the awkwardness that had plagued them earlier.

"So do you think we're crazy for seeing each other?" Caroline asked.

"I don't know. I really hadn't thought about it much. I know that after our first encounter, it surely wasn't anything that I expected or looked for," Caleb replied.

Caroline let out a giggle. "Me either. Especially since I tried to run you off the ranch. I would have succeeded if you weren't so wily in backing me into corners," she said before taking another sip of wine.

"We didn't exactly hit it off," he said and smiled at the memory.

"I knew you'd be trouble and I was right. Having a good looking man around is just asking for it," Caroline said. The wine had removed her inhibitions and she felt young and lighthearted again like she had in the old days.

Caleb leaned over and lightly kissed Caroline. She wrapped her arms around him and pulled him over onto her. Encouraged by her actions, Caleb kissed her with all the passion that had been simmering in him for way too long. They began necking with the desperation of two people that had been lonely for years. Caleb moved his hand over and cupped Caroline's breast. He knew he shouldn't, but he couldn't help himself. Half expecting all hell to break loose, Caroline surprised him by quickly unfastening the three buttons at the front of her dress.

"Caleb, I need you," Caroline implored.

∞

Joey and Claire were chatting at the kitchen table while drinking coffee after their trip to town to dine at the hotel. Both had feasted on T-bone steaks and polished the meal off with generous portions of apple pie. Drinking coffee was their attempt at warding off the need for naps that the lethargy of full stomachs had brought on them. The day had been a success. After declaring their intentions towards each other, the couple had dropped any pretense of formality in public and behaved as two people smitten in each other's company.

Caroline entered the house carrying the picnic basket, blanket, and her rifle. She walked into the kitchen and set the items down before plopping into a chair beside Joey.

"Did you have a nice time?" Claire asked her daughter.

"I did. We had a real good time today," Caroline said without any enthusiasm.

Sensing that Caroline needed to talk with her mother, Joey said, "I guess I've loafed enough for one day. I think I'll take me a ride and have a look around the ranch. You ladies have a nice rest of the day." As he stood, Joey contemplated kissing Claire goodbye, but couldn't bring himself to show any such affection in front of Caroline. He tipped his hat, gave Claire a furtive wink, and let himself out of the house.

"What's the matter? Now that you and Caleb spent the day together, was it not all that you hoped for?" Claire asked.

"No, that's not it," Caroline replied.

"Well, what is it then?" Claire persisted.

"I don't know," Caroline said with bewilderment.

"Sure you do. If you don't want to talk about it, just say so," Claire said.

Caroline looked up from the table at her mother and let out a sigh. "Mother, I've fallen in love with Caleb. And I'm mean really in love. I don't know how it happened - I really don't. I didn't think I even liked him. He caught my attention the first time that I saw him, but there was something about his ways that annoyed me. I didn't bargain for this," she said with exasperation.

"So love is a bad thing?" Claire asked.

"What if he turns out to be like George? I didn't do too well the first time I fell in love. I can't put myself through that again," Caroline said.

"For goodness sakes, Caroline. Caleb has done more work around here in the short time that he's been here than George did the entire time you were married. I never said anything back then, but I always had misgivings about him. I certainly don't feel that way about Caleb. Is there anything about Caleb that reminds you of George?" Claire demanded.

"No, not a thing," Caroline said quietly.

"Well, quit worrying then and just enjoy your time together. You've acted happier in the last couple of weeks than I have seen in forever. It's not a crime to be happy. If nothing else comes from it, you've at least learned that life goes on after a bad marriage," Claire said.

Caroline smiled sheepishly. "Thanks. I needed to hear that. Maybe I think too much. How was your day?" she asked.

"We had a lovely time. I guess you could say that we are officially courting. At Joey's and my ages, it's not like buying that dress that you've had your eye on forever, but it certainly is like pulling the one from the chifforobe that you always wear because it makes you feel good and is comfortable," Claire said.

Giggling, Caroline said, "That doesn't sound much like *Romeo and Juliet*, but I'm happy for you."

"Just remember that they died young. I'm still planning on being around long enough to enjoy some grandchildren," Claire said.

Caroline blushed and averted her eyes down towards the table. "Let's not get ahead of ourselves. I'm going to change clothes and rest for a while," she said before walking towards her room.

Chapter 22

Having skipped going to town the previous week, Caroline needed to make her usual Wednesday trip to get supplies. She spotted Dan as she scampered out of the house and recruited him to help her hitch the horses to the buckboard.

Joey came out of the bunkhouse and walked over to the wagon. "Are you planning on making a trip to town?' he asked Caroline.

"Yes, it's Wednesday and we're running low on about everything. We're feeding a couple more people than we used to around here," Caroline replied.

"Who's going with you?" Joey inquired.

"I wasn't planning on taking anybody. You and Mother went to town on Sunday. I'm beginning to think that Nathan is being sincere," she answered.

"That's the point - I was with your mother. I doubt even Nathan Horn would pull something on a Sunday after making a point of talking to us at the church," he responded.

"Joey, I'm a big girl. I can take care of myself," Caroline insisted.

"I really don't think you should go alone," Joey said as he helped Caroline get the harness on a horse.

"Is this what it has come to, you think you are in charge now that you and Mother are getting close?" she said irritably.

"Caroline, be fair. You know that I'm only concerned for your welfare," Joey responded.

Caleb walked up beside Joey. "What are you two arguing about?" he asked.

"Joey doesn't think I should go to town alone," Caroline snapped.

"Well, I don't either. Have you already forgotten what's gone on around here? Nathan Horn doesn't strike me as someone that would give up that easily," Caleb said.

"Fine. Why don't you and Joey both ride with me? You can guard both sides of the road that way," she said sarcastically.

"That's a good idea. Now you're talking some sense. I need to get another pair of pants and a couple of shirts anyways," Caleb said.

Caroline threw her hands into the air and shook her head. "Suit yourself, but you two can ride your horses. When we get to town, I'll go in first and then you can follow after me. You can wait for me in the saloon. I'll not have the whole town thinking that I need a couple of babysitters," she said.

Caleb grinned at Joey and gave him a wink. "Whatever makes you happy," he said.

"You two don't want to know what would make me happy right about now," Caroline said as she climbed aboard the wagon and sat with her arms crossed watching the men finish the hitching.

After retrieving their horses from the barn, Joey and Caleb set out with Caroline towards town. Caroline's mood softened considerably as they traveled and her mind turned to the ranch.

"Do you think I should try to see Colonel Devin and invite him out to see our horses?" Caroline asked Joey.

"I think I'd wait a couple of weeks. We're still behind on the training and we need to shoot guns from the saddle yet. I'd rather make a good first impression," Joey answered.

"You are probably right. I wish the fort would quit changing commanders," Caroline said.

"I wouldn't count on that," Joey said.

"How are your ribs feeling?" Caroline asked.

"Pretty good. I only notice any pain when I get jarred real good," Joey replied.

Deciding that the time had come to broach the subject of Joey and her mother, Caroline said, "Mother seems to be walking on the clouds since Sunday."

"We had us a real nice time and certainly enjoy each other's company. I know you don't like it much. Truth be told, I find the whole thing quite surprising. It was nothing that I ever planned," Joey said.

"As long as she is happy, I'm fine with whatever goes on between you two. I guess I've come to realize that life goes on and you have to change with it," Caroline said.

Feeling left out and nearly invisible, Caleb said, "You're going to ruin your reputation if you start talking like that."

As Caroline looked up from the wagon at Caleb, she smiled and said, "You are to blame for most of this. If I ever have a change of heart, I'm coming for you for doing this to me and for Joey for bringing you here."

Caleb began reminiscing about training horses with his father back in Tennessee as the trio continued on their journey towards town. They reached an area where the land flattened out in a long wide pass with foothills on either side of the road. As they traveled about halfway down the stretch, three riders charged out of the trees on the side of one of the hills.

"They've been waiting for you. Take off," Caleb yelled to Caroline as he pulled his Winchester from its scabbard.

Caroline grabbed the whip and popped the rears of the horses, causing the animals to bolt into a run. The riders were still a good two hundred yards away and coming at a full gallop as the buckboard gained speed.

"What do you think we should do?" Caleb asked.

"Let's hold our ground until they get closer. We can take a shot at them and then we'd better follow Caroline," Joey replied.

"I don't want her to get out of sight or chance those men getting past us. They could have stationed someone up ahead too," Caleb said.

As the riders closed to within a hundred yards, Joey said, "Let them have it."

The riders ducked behind their horses and angled off a straight course when they saw the rifles raised in their direction. Caleb and Joey tried to line up a shot, firing in a vain attempt to bring down their targets.

"Let's get out of here," Caleb yelled as he spun his horse and spurred it into a gallop.

Caroline had never driven a wagon at such speed. She felt as if she were going faster than when she rode Buddy at a hard gallop. Maintaining control of the buckboard seemed a lot scarier than any bronco that she had ever attempted to ride. Just staying on the seat took a herculean effort. The wagon wheels hit a bump in the road and Caroline could feel herself launched towards the sky. With catlike reflexes, she managed to snag the backrest of the seat to save herself from flying from the wagon, but lost the reins in the process. She watched helplessly as the horses veered sharply off the road. The wagon tipped up onto two wheels. Caroline tried to shift her body to bring the buckboard back to the ground, but her small size had no effect. As the wagon tipped onto its side, Caroline catapulted through the air.

Caleb and Joey watched in horror as the wagon overturned and Caroline appeared as if she were fired from a cannon. The men chasing after them began shooting, but neither noticed nor cared. Getting to Caroline was all that mattered. They made it to the wagon and jumped from their horses before the animals had come to a stop. The riders were boring down on Caleb and Joey as they took cover behind the wagon and aimed their rifles. Both men fired upon the lead rider, knocking him out of the saddle and sending him bouncing across the ground like a tossed doll. The two remaining men cut their horses hard in opposite directions in an attempt to circle behind the wagon. Joey took a shot at the man nearest him and missed. The rider on Caleb's side turned his horse straight towards Caroline's prone body. Caleb dashed to Caroline and stood over her as the charging horseman fired upon him. Taking aim at the rider's horse, Caleb shot his Winchester as fast as he could cock the gun and fire. As the horse began to stumble from its injuries, a shot knocked Caleb to the ground. The horse collapsed twenty yards away, sending the rider crashing into the ground. Caleb forced himself up and hobbled towards the man on the ground. He recognized his assailant as the man that he had beaten up in the bar that Nathan had referred to as Eddie. As Eddie sat up and drew his revolver, Caleb gripped his rifle by the barrel and swung the butt into the pistol. The revolver flew through the air as Eddie let out a scream.

"How did you know we were here?" Caleb hollered.

"Go to hell," Eddie yelled.

Caleb clubbed the rifle into Eddie's chest, knocking the ranch hand onto his back. The sound of rapidly fired shots diverted Caleb's attention and he looked up to see the third man hightailing it in a retreat while Joey tried to shoot him. The rider made it out of range and disappeared out of sight.

"Talk," Caleb shouted as he crashed the rifle into Eddie's knee.

Eddie let out a shriek of pain. "Nathan and everybody else knew that she comes to town on Wednesday. We were here last week waiting too," he said.

"You were going to run her over with your horse while she lay there helpless on the ground," Caleb accused him.

Smiling through teeth clenched in pain, Eddie said, "After all you put me through lately, do you really think I give a damn? She was worth an extra hundred bucks if I was the one that killed her," he said.

Caleb raised the rifle above his head and brought it down like an axe on top of Eddie's skull. The blow sounded like a melon bursting. He bashed his nemesis's head two more times. The second blow sent an eye shooting out of its socket. Before Caleb could swing his rifle again, Joey came running up and tackled him.

"Enough," Joey yelled from atop Caleb.

Seeing Joey sprawled on top of him, Caleb came to his senses. "We have to check on Caroline," he said as he shoved Joey off him. He got to his feet and limped to her. "See if she's breathing. I don't think I can do it."

Joey gently rolled Caroline onto her back. A nasty looking knot had already formed on her forehead. Putting his fingers against her neck, Joey checked for a pulse and lowered his head to listen for sounds of breathing. "She's alive. Her breathing sounds okay," he said.

"I'll get the horses and you can hand her up to me," Caleb said.

"Slow down. You're not thinking straight. Let's see if the wagon is busted first. We can turn it over and straighten out the harness. If Caroline has internal injuries, you could kill her trying to carry her on horseback. And we need to see how badly you're hurt," Joey said.

Caleb looked at his blood soaked pants, realizing for the first time that he had been shot. He reached down and stuck his index finger into the entrance and then the exit wound. The bullet had entered his thigh about an inch in from the outside of his leg, passing through the muscle and exiting. "I'll be fine. Let's get busy," he said.

"Tie your bandana around it. That'll help with the bleeding," Joey ordered.

After Caleb tied his kerchief around his leg, the two men examined the wagon. The buckboard had survived its spill with only a cracked sideboard. They righted the wagon and began untangling the harness. The collars and girths were twisted on the horses and the traces had come unhooked. Caleb was forced to hold the heads of the jittery animals while Joey worked on the harness.

"I think that about does it. Get in the back and I'll hand Caroline to you," Joey said as he reattached the last trace.

Retrieving his rifle, Caleb cleaned the blood off the gun's butt using grass and reloaded its magazine before climbing into the back of the wagon. Joey gently lifted Caroline and carried her to the back of the buckboard. Caleb paused a moment to look at Caroline as he took her in his arms and brushed some dirt off her cheek. He scooted towards the front of the wagon and held Caroline like a baby.

Once Joey finished tying their horses behind the wagon, he climbed onto the seat. "Are you ready?" he asked.

"Let's get going. She has me worried sick," Caleb answered.

With a gentle flick of the reins, they resumed their trip to town. Joey did his best to maneuver around potholes and bumps, but the ride still proved jarring. Caleb's tailbone suffered most of the jolts as he cradled Caroline's head in his arms. One particular bump bounced the wagon hard. Caroline opened her eyes and looked up at Caleb.

"What happened?" Caroline asked groggily.

Hearing Caroline speak made Caleb go weak. He felt as if he would melt onto the floorboard and had to steel his emotions in order to find his voice. "You were thrown from the wagon," he replied.

"Am I going to die?" she asked.

"No, no. You just have a bump on your head. I need you to tell me if you hurt anywhere else," Caleb said.

Caroline seemed to need a moment to process the request. She raised her arms and twiddled her fingers before lifting her legs. "I don't think so," she said.

"Good. You're going to be fine," he reassured her.

"We were being chased," Caroline said absently.

"Yes, Joey and I got two of them. One of them got away. Don't worry. You're safe now," Caleb reassured her.

"I know," she said.

"Caroline, I love you," Caleb said as his emotions overwhelmed him.

"I love you too," Caroline said before drifting off.

"Joey, I think she's going to be okay," Caleb called out.

"I think so. We're about there," Joey replied.

Joey drove the wagon to the door of the doctor's office and jumped down from it. Running to the back of the buckboard, he waited as Caleb slid himself to the rear.

"You better let me carry her in case your leg gives out on you," Joey said.

Caleb handed Caroline to Joey and limped to the door to open it. Inside they found Doctor August Albright sitting at his desk reading a newspaper. The doctor looked to be in his mid-forties with hair graying at the temples and a kindly expression. He removed his spectacles and set them down on top of his paper.

"What do we have here?" the doctor asked.

"She was thrown from the wagon and has a knot on her forehead. She woke up long enough to tell me that she didn't think she was hurt anywhere else," Caleb answered.

"Set her on the bed," Doctor Albright instructed.

Joey placed Caroline on the cot and stepped back. The doctor pulled a curtain between himself and the two men and began removing Caroline's clothes. Once he had her undressed, the doctor methodically checked her limbs for broken bones before retrieving smelling salts from a cabinet. He held the salts under her nose until Caroline began batting her eyes rapidly. She opened them with a start.

"Hello, Caroline. I haven't seen you in a while. How do you feel?" the doctor asked.

Caroline thought for a moment before answering. "My head is pounding," she said.

"Tell me if this hurts," Doctor Albright said as he pushed on her stomach and abdomen.

"Not anywhere," she said when he stopped.

The doctor covered Caroline with a sheet and opened the curtain. He leaned over and examined Caroline's eyes.

"You have a concussion, but otherwise I think you are fine. You were lucky. I've seen more than one person come through that door after being thrown from a wagon that had more broken pieces than a smashed bottle," the doctor said as he retrieved a tincture of willow bark. He poured the liquid into a spoon and shoved it into Caroline's mouth. Caroline scrunched up her face at the taste. "That should help your headache."

Caleb pulled his hat from his head and held it nervously in his hands. "Do you think she's going to be okay?" he asked anxiously.

"I do. She needs to stay here for the night and we will see how she is in the morning," Doc Albright answered.

"Caleb, you are shot," Caroline said as she raised her head from the pillow.

"I'm okay. It's nothing," Caleb said.

"Young man, I need to treat your leg. A good-looking buck like you doesn't want to get gangrene and have to hop around on one leg the rest of your life. I have a feeling that Caroline might want a dance or two from you," the doctor said, giving Caleb a wink.

Joey placed his hat back on his head and stood. "I'm going to go tell someone at the fort what happened and let them know there's bodies to retrieve," he said.

"You probably need to go get Claire when you're done. I'm sure she'll want to stay with Caroline tonight and we need to get home afterwards. We're finishing this tomorrow," Caleb said.

Chapter 23

Before Caleb and Joey left the doctor's office, Caroline seemed more like her usual self. She had slept most of the time, but when awake, she no longer appeared as if she were in a complete daze. Claire, on the other hand, had been a nervous wreck and the doctor had plied her with two glasses of brandy to calm her nerves. Once Caleb and Joey were satisfied that the women would be fine without them, they said their goodbyes and headed home.

Joey had been to the Horn ranch several times, and with his knowledge of the layout of place, they devised a plan of attack during their ride. The rest of the crew anxiously greeted them back at the bunkhouse. Caleb and Joey had to recount the day's events before exhaustion kicked in and they crawled into their bunks for the evening.

The aching in Caleb's leg had caused him a rough night of sleep. Dr. Albright, having witnessed the horrors of addiction, seldom administered anything stronger than willow bark tincture and that medicine had only managed to knock the edge off Caleb's pain. At three-thirty in the morning, Caleb tried to crawl out of bed and found his leg so stiff that he had to lift it with his hands to get it to the floor. He willed himself to stand and began pacing the floor to loosen up his limb. The noise woke up the other ranch hands, but nobody dared complain after the events of the previous day. Joey got up, lit the oil lamps, and started fixing breakfast for the crew as Caleb continued to walk the length of the bunkhouse. By the time the eggs, bacon, and ham had cooked, Caleb had gone from dragging his leg to walking with a limp.

As they passed the food around the table, Joey asked, "How bad are you?"

"I'm ready to ride and see what the day has in store," Caleb said solemnly.

"So do you still think that the two of us should ride to Horn's place and take on however many men he has?" Joey asked.

"Joey, I'm not asking you to go, but I'm going one way or another," Caleb replied.

"You know I wouldn't let you go by yourself. I just think we have a tall task in front of us," Joey said.

After taking a sip of coffee, Dan set his cup down and said, "I'll go too."

"Dan, if Caleb and I don't make it back, I'm counting on you to look after Caroline and Claire. They'll need you," Joey said.

Dan nodded his head soberly.

"I guess it's settled then," Caleb said before taking a bite of egg.

Breakfast turned into a somber affair with the burdens of the day weighing heavily on the men. Dan, Lucky, and Reese made a hasty retreat from the bunkhouse to do chores by lamplight, leaving Caleb and Joey sitting at the table sipping coffee.

"Do you want to go to town first and see Caroline before we do this? We could wait until tomorrow morning," Joey suggested.

"Caroline knows how I feel about her now and we had our goodbye. It would just be awkward if we went this morning. If I'm going to die, I'd just as soon get it over with instead of thinking about it," Caleb replied.

Joey rubbed his finger around the brim of his cup and nodded his head. "I'm sorry I ever got you into this mess. You'd be better off if we never crossed paths," Joey said.

Smiling, Caleb let out a sigh. "We're not dead yet and I wouldn't change a thing except for Caroline getting hurt. I feel more alive than I have in a long time," he said before holding out his hand and shaking with Joey. "You've become a brother to me. I wouldn't have missed this for the world."

"I feel the same about you," Joey said.

Caleb tugged on the leather bracelet that Alice had given him. "Before I found you I met this old lady on the trail. She fed me and gave me this bracelet. She was real mysterious and said that she thought I'd find love again and that better days were ahead. Let's hope she meant they were supposed to last more than a couple of weeks," he said.

"Life is a funny thing. Sometimes a chance meeting can change your whole life. If I hadn't been robbed, we would have never met and you wouldn't have ever known Caroline even existed," Joey mused.

Grinning, Caleb said, "I bet you never thought you'd be courting Claire either."

"No, hardly. I never would have even dared to consider such a thing if Claire hadn't made her interest known to me," Joey said.

"Do you think Nathan and his men will be waiting for us?" Caleb asked.

"I don't know what to think after yesterday. Did they think that the rest of us would just quit if they killed Caroline?" Joey asked.

"I don't know, but if they did, they made a serious misjudgment," Caleb said.

"You're going to need to keep your head about you and not get all worked up on revenge," Joey said.

"I'm not going to let you down. We better get started so we beat first light," Caleb said as he braced his hands against the table to aid himself in standing.

Joey walked to the old wardrobe and retrieved the last of the dynamite. He stuck the two sticks, a cap, and some left over fuse in an oiled leather pouch before following Caleb out the door.

Caleb decided that he needed a horse that he could count on to be fast and trustworthy so he saddled Leif. Joey chose the horse he'd ridden to Illinois. The two men headed out in the dark for the Horn ranch. Figuring that they would be less likely to be discovered coming from the north, the two men made a wide arc around the ranch. They ended up a little over a quarter of a mile above the Horn residence at a creek that ran past the ranch's bunkhouse. Joey hid the horses in a pine grove before he and Caleb slid down the four-foot bank into the creek bed.

"There's not enough neatsfoot oil in the world to keep boots dry walking in a creek. I hate getting my feet wet," Caleb whispered as they began wading down the three-inch deep creek.

"Me and you both. And I hate the way my boots shrink and hurt my feet for a couple of days afterwards," Joey replied.

By the time Caleb and Joey slogged down to the bunkhouse, twilight made its first appearance to the east. The remnants of a campfire out in the yard produced enough glow to see a guard sleeping in a chair. They crouched down against the side of the creek bank and waited for more light. Time seemed to move as slowly as the languid creek water while watching the eastern horizon. Finally, the gray morning sky produced enough light to see the sights on their rifles and to discern objects.

"Let's get the party started," Caleb whispered as he removed the sticks of dynamite from the pouch and attached the cap and fuse.

The side of the bunkhouse ran parallel to the creek with a window towards each end. Caleb scampered up the bank and limped towards the rear window. Looking through the glass, the darkness made it impossible to see anything inside the structure. With a strike of a match on his boot heel, Caleb lit the fuse and watched it burn halfway down before grabbing his revolver and breaking the glass. He tossed the sticks through the window and hobbled back to the creek as fast as his leg would allow. The two men ducked their heads just before the explosion ripped through the stillness of the morning. A peek over the bank revealed the rear of the bunkhouse had disintegrated. A moment later, Frankie Myers and three other armed cowboys stumbled from the front of the building while the guard ran around his campfire trying to figure out what had just happened.

"Here we go," Joey said as he raised his Winchester.

Caleb and Joey fired their rifles, knocking two ranch hands to the ground. The other three men spun towards the creek and shot their guns wildly as Caleb and Joey hid below the bank. Popping back up, Caleb and Joey sent another cowboy into to the dirt with their second volley. In desperation, Frankie and the guard retreated behind the bunkhouse.

"I'm going after them," Caleb said as he pulled his Colt from the holster.

"I'm with you," Joey said as he retrieved his revolver.

Caleb and Joey hustled to the corner of the bunkhouse with their rifle in one hand and their revolver in the other and peeked around the corner. They caught a glimpse of the two cowboys disappearing into the barn.

"That's not good," Joey said.

"I'd burn it to the ground if not for killing the horses," Caleb said.

"I'll take the rear and you take the front. Keep an eye out on the house. Nathan and Milo are probably scrambling for their guns," Joey said.

Caleb entered the barn and squatted next to a stall as his eyes adjusted to the darkness. As he scanned the building for any sign of the men, Joey appeared at the other end of the barn. He gave Joey a shrug sign. Joey motioned for them to start checking each stall. One of them would make a quick look into a stall while the other kept on eye on all the others stall. They methodically worked their way down the hall until meeting in the middle.

"They have to be in the loft," Joey said, pointing to the steps leading upstairs.

"Let's run the horses into the corral. We can throw some hay into the stairwell and light it. If we try to go up those steps, we'd last about as long as ice in hell. We'll get them when they jump out the sides," Caleb said.

"I guess asking them to come down is out of the question," Joey said in an attempt to find some humor in the situation.

"I'm sure Frankie would love that," Caleb said as opened a stall and led a horse out into the hallway.

Stall by stall, they pulled out the horses and ran the animals out the back entrance. Caleb began gathering hay from the stalls and throwing it into the stairwell. Joey watched the top of the stairs with his revolver drawn, ready for an attack from the two men.

A man screamed from outside the barn. "I broke my leg," he hollered.

"They already jumped out," Caleb said and ran out the front door before Joey could grab him.

Two shots sent Caleb diving back into the barn.

"I told you to keep your head about you. I don't know how you ever survived the war. Did they hit you?" Joey yelled.

"No, but those shots were from the house," Caleb said as he snuck a glance outside by cracking the door.

One of the ranch hands was making a dash for the house. Caleb raised his rifle and fired. The man kept on running but looked as if his legs were going faster than his body. He ran a few more steps and landed face first in the grass.

"Did you get one?" Joey asked.

"Yup. We're down to the one with the broken leg and I guess Nathan and Milo in the house," Caleb answered as he reloaded his rifle.

"We're going to get killed trying to shoot from behind that barn door. It's not going to stop a bullet," Joey said.

"Maybe I can get a shot from the loft without being spotted," Caleb suggested.

All the walking and running had Caleb's leg bleeding again and made his limp noticeably more pronounced. He labored to walk up the stairs and had to use his rifle as a cane. Joey followed him into the loft.

Caleb opened the small door on the side of the barn just enough to see the house. Two men manned windows with their rifles pointed towards the barn.

Plopping down onto his butt, Caleb said, "They don't see us. They're concentrating too hard on the front of the barn. Do you think you can shoot over me?"

"I'll do anything to get this over with," Joey replied as he got onto his knees.

"I'll take the one on the left. Tell me when you have a bead," Caleb said.

"Ready," Joey said.

"On the count of three. One, two, three," Caleb counted calmly.

The two Winchesters roared with deafening noise. Both men winced from the pain to their ears.

"I got mine," Joey said.

"So did I," Caleb responded as he swung the door wide open. He spotted Frankie Myers crawling away towards a shed. "Hey, Frankie, where are you going?"

Frankie rolled onto his back and raised his revolver with his wobbly left arm. As he struggled to aim his pistol, a bullet from Caleb's rifle tore into the cowboy's heart. His head flopped back onto the ground and his gun discharged towards the sky.

"Let's go see what we find in the house," Joey said grimly.

"We're still alive," Caleb remarked

The two men were halfway to the house when Caleb's leg gave out on him. He went down on one knee and had to use his hands to steady himself.

"I'll go see if they're dead. You stay here," Joey said.

"No, I want to see it for myself. Help me, please," Caleb pleaded.

Joey pulled him to his feet and Caleb put his arm over Joey's shoulders. They walked at a turtle's pace to the front door. Joey tried the door and found it locked. He raised his leg and smashed his boot heel into the door, sending it crashing open. They hobbled in through the entrance and were caught unprepared for a blood-soaked Nathan sitting against a wall with a rifle. The rancher grappled to aim his gun at them. Joey shoved Caleb to the floor and dived on top of him as Nathan fired a shot. Joey didn't move and his weight had Caleb pinned. Caleb managed to fling his partner to the side and drew his revolver as Nathan struggled to chamber another cartridge. With military trained precision, Caleb emptied his Colt into the rancher. As each bullet struck Nathan, he flinched but continued to attempt to cock his rifle until his head finally dropped onto his chest.

"Joey, are you okay?" Caleb hollered.

A gasping sound was the only response that Caleb heard. He rolled over to see Joey's eyes bulging and his mouth wide open fighting for air.

"Oh, God, this can't happen now. Don't you dare die on me," Caleb said as he vainly searched for a wound on his friend.

"Landed ... on ... your ... hip ... Got ... air ... knocked ... out ..." Joey managed to say.

"Good God, you scared the devil out of me," Caleb said unsympathetically as he wacked Joey on the shoulder.

Caleb looked over towards a window and saw Milo sprawled out near it. The young man had taken a bullet to the head and probably died before hitting the floor. Caleb wished that he could feel some remorse for the death of Milo, but he just couldn't summon up any compassion. The whole idea of ruining the Langley ranch had been folly and the Horn family had paid their due for the mistake.

After getting his wind back, Joey said, "See if I ever try to save your life again you ungrateful turd."

The stress of the last two days gave way and the two men began laughing hysterically. They slapped at their legs and carried on until they wiped tears from their eyes. Only the sudden slumping over of Nathan's body caused the giggling to die out.

Caleb pulled off his hat and ran his fingers through his hair. He let out a sigh and said, "We killed seven men today."

"I know we did. It's like I told you when we crossed paths with that horse thief on the trail - out here, a man has to protect what's his. If we had let Caroline go to town by herself, she'd be dead now. It's just the way things are," Joey said.

"Will the army look into this?" Caleb asked.

"My guess it that they'll put two and two together and leave things alone now that the score is settled. The army doesn't like to concern itself with civilian feuds unless they have no choice. They are more worried about keeping the Indians in line," Joey said as he stood. He held out his arm and helped pull Caleb to his feet. "I'm going to turn the horses in the corral loose and then go get our horses. You can sit on the porch until I get back."

Hobbling towards the door, Caleb said, "We do make a pretty good team."

Chapter 24

By the time that Caleb and Joey made it back to the ranch, Caleb's blood loss, physical exertion, and lack of sleep had him ready to crawl into his bunk and nap for hours. Joey would have none of it. He filled a pan with water and started heating it.

"I'm cleaning your wound like the doctor showed me and dousing it with iodine before you jump into bed. We've both seen men die from dirty wounds and I won't sit back and watch that happen. Now shuck those pants," Joey demanded.

Caleb debated whether to argue the point, but felt so weary that he couldn't summon up the will to try. "I told you that I thought of you as a brother, not my mother," he said as he took off his pants.

With the pan of water, a rag, and a bar of soap in hand, Joey walked over and began scrubbing around the wound. "I don't see any festering and the color looks good," he said as he worked.

"Don't much matter if you kill me from the pain you're causing," Caleb said as he winced and gritted his teeth.

"I didn't know you were such a sissy. If you want real pain, try having some cracked ribs," Joey said as he retrieved the bottle of iodine and doused the wound.

"Yeah, lying around the boss's house looked unbearable," Caleb responded.

"Love is making you plume witty," Joey said as he finished by redressing the wounds with a clean bandage.

Grabbing his last pair of clean trousers, Caleb pulled them on and sat down on his bunk. "I got to get some sleep. I haven't been this weary since the war," he said.

"I'm going to take a nap too. We earned our keep today," Joey said as he walked towards his bed.

The two men were snoring in a matter of minutes. Dan looked in on them at noon and decided that he and the rest of the crew best forego lunch to let them sleep.

In the early afternoon, Caleb felt his sleep being interrupted by someone lightly shaking him. He jumped with a start as he awakened, opening his eyes to see Caroline bent over him with Claire by her side.

"Hello, sleepyhead. I didn't know I was paying you to snooze," Caroline teased.

"Caroline, how are you feeling?" Caleb asked as he tried to get his senses about him. He noticed that she still had a bump on her head and some bruising, but looked better than when he last saw her.

"I'm okay. Doctor Albright said I could go home after I kept breakfast down. I had a rough evening of vomiting after you and Joey left. I still feel a little woozy and the wagon ride proved a bit rough. How are you feeling?" she said.

"I'm fine. I just needed some rest after this morning," Caleb replied.

The voices awakened Joey and he sat up on his bed. "The queen and princess have returned," he said.

Claire walked over to Joey and bent over, boldly kissing him on the lips. "What happened this morning?" she asked.

"Nathan and all his men are gone. We took care of all of them. It's over," Joey said.

"Oh, my," Claire said. She walked to the table, pulled a chair over to Joey, and sat down on it. "I hate this."

"Claire, we didn't have a choice. They tried to kill Caroline," Joey said.

"I know, but it doesn't make this whole thing any less sad. I am happy that it's over with," Claire said.

Caleb stood and began walking the stiffness back out of his leg. The others watched him with expressions of sympathy that he did not covet. "It just takes a minute to get my leg loosened up. It's not that bad," he said.

"We have Grandpa Langley's old cane in the house. You need to use it for a few days," Caroline suggested.

"I'm not an old man and I don't need any cane," Caleb said disgustedly.

"Yes, you do. Your leg will heal quicker if you're not putting such a strain on it. Don't be vain and pigheaded," Caroline said.

Caleb started to object but before he could speak, Claire stood abruptly and said, "You two come with us. I'll fix you a good meal while Caroline finds the cane." She looked directly at Caleb with her practiced motherly look that meant she had heard enough.

"I am hungry," Caleb said with a sheepish grin.

"Let's go then," Claire said before heading for the door. She stopped suddenly and spun towards the others. "I do want the both of you to know how grateful I am. You saved the ranch and Caroline. I really don't know what we would have done without either of you."

Joey walked over to Claire and put his arm around her shoulders. "You two may be paying us back for a long time," he said and winked at Caleb.

Claire reached over and patted Joey's stomach. "Don't expect to hear any complaints from me," she said.

Caroline looked down at the floor, too embarrassed to make eye contact with anyone after Joey and her mother's innuendos. She could feel her ears turning red. In a different situation, she would have been upset and spoken her piece, but too much had gone on in the last couple of days to even consider being mad with a little frisky behavior.

The four of them walked to the house and Claire began preparing a meal. While Caroline searched for the cane and Claire parboiled the steaks to remove the excess salt, there came a knock on the door. Claire grabbed a towel and dried her hands as she walked to the front of the house. She opened the door to find Captain Tyrone Willis.

Captain Willis had served at Fort Laramie for years. His knowledge of the area and his loyalty to his superiors had indebted him to the ever changing list of commanders at the fort. The captain had been a friend of Claire's husband Jackson and always appreciated the quality of the horses the ranch had supplied the army. He had remained a steadfast proponent for the ranch even after Jackson's death.

"Captain Willis, what brings you out here?" Claire asked as she slung her towel over her shoulder.

The captain removed his hat and nodded his head in greeting. "Hello, Mrs. Langley. I was ordered to interrogate Nathan Horn after the incident that Joey reported concerning Caroline yesterday. When I went to his ranch, I found him, his son, and five ranch hands dead. I felt compelled to stop in and ask you if you knew anything about their deaths," the captain said.

"I just got home from the doctor's office a little while ago," Claire answered.

"What about the men that work for you?" Captain Willis questioned.

"I never asked any of my men to do such a thing," Claire replied in her dance around the truth.

"Do you think that some of them might have taken their own initiative while you were gone and done it?" the captain asked.

"Captain Willis, I hire men for their abilities with horses, not guns," she said.

"I see," the captain said as he studied Claire. "I'm guessing that somebody decided that trying to kill a woman crossed a line and was a capital offense."

"I can't say that I would disagree with them, especially considering that that woman was my daughter. Would you?" Claire asked.

'No, ma'am, I don't think that I would. You have a nice day," Captain Willis said.

"Thank you. And you do the same. Tell the commander that we should have some horses ready in a couple of weeks if he would like to accompany you to see them," Claire said.

"Yes, ma'am," the captain said before putting on his hat and adjusting it to his satisfaction. He turned and walked towards his horse.

Claire walked back into the kitchen. "That was Captain Willis. I don't think the army will look any further into Nathan's death," she announced.

"I didn't figure they'd want to get in the middle of this. It would just bring more attention to the fact that it happened under their watch," Joey said.

Caroline came walking into the kitchen with the cane. She was stooped over and using it as if she were an old woman. "I finally found it in the back of the wardrobe in the spare bedroom," she said as she handed it to Caleb.

"You're just a hoot," Caleb said as he took the walking stick.

While forking the steaks from the boiling water into the skillet, Claire said, "Tomorrow, this ranch should be able to get back to concentrating on the horses. I told the captain that we would have some ready for him to see in a couple of weeks."

"Working with horses will seem like a day off," Joey said.

Caleb ran his hand down the smoothly sanded cane, smiling as he thought about what he was about to say. "I'm sure that Caroline will find a way to take the joy out of it," he said.

With her hands on her hips, Caroline smirked as she looked at Caleb. Her head was beginning to hurt, but she didn't care. The relief in knowing that the troubles were over had put her in a fine mood. She felt as carefree as a bird and had an urge to be as audacious as her mother had been earlier. Striding towards Caleb, she sat down on his good leg and wrapped her arms around his neck. "That all depends on what you are willing to do to keep me happy," she said before planting a big kiss on his lips.

Chapter 25

Nils and Olivia Berg rode into Chalksville on their buckboard wagon. The couple always wore their good clothes to town and treated the trip as if out for a Sunday ride. After stopping in front of the general store, Nils patiently climbed down and helped Olivia from the wagon. Their grandson, Tyler, had turned four and the family planned a dinner that evening. Olivia intended to buy Tyler a tin whistle and candy for both of the children as well as some other things for the meal. Nils climbed back onto the wagon and headed for the post office. He was pleased to find a letter from his sister Ingrid when he got there.

His sister had married a little later in life when a Kentucky gentleman had come to buy a horse from Nils. The two had been smitten with each other at first sight and soon married. Caleb and Britt had been heartbroken when their doting Aunt Ingrid had moved to Kentucky, but had spent parts of each summer with her and her husband well into their teens.

Nils shoved the letter into his pocket and continued with his errands around town. When he returned to the general store, he found Olivia standing outside waiting for him with her purchases.

"You are getting slow in your old age," Olivia teased.

As Nils placed Olivia's things in the back of the buckboard, he said, "I always have to play Walter a couple of games of checkers. He's convinced that he will beat me someday and it hasn't happened yet."

"You should let him win once in a while," Olivia chided her husband as he helped her onto the seat.

"You know me too well for that to happen. I'm making him a better player by beating him," Nils said before walking around the wagon and climbing aboard it.

On the way home, "Olivia asked, "Did we have any mail?"

"I almost forgot. Here's a letter from Ingrid," Nils replied as he handed the envelope to Olivia.

"They need to come for a visit," Olivia said as she opened the letter. She read the first page from her sister-in-law and turned to the second. "Oh my goodness, the rest of it is from Caleb."

"Read it to me," Nils said anxiously as he pulled the reins on the horses until the wagon stopped.

"Dear Daddy, Momma, and Britt, I hope this letter finds you all well. I sent it to Aunt Ingrid for fear the sheriff has your mail watched. I am working on a horse ranch in Fort Laramie in the Wyoming Territory. I helped out a man named Joey Clemson on the trail and he brought me here. A mother and daughter run the ranch. When I first arrived, they were having trouble with another rancher. That is all resolved now. The west is not as civilized as back home and a man has to defend what is his. Daddy will be interested to know that they breed wild mustangs to their stallions and then train the offspring for army and cattle horses. We have used Leif on some of the mustangs. I am excited to see what his foals look like next year. I still feel awful for the predicament that I left you all in. I hope things have been resolved and you have been able to go on with your life. Britt, I hope and pray that you bear me no ill will and that you are not struggling with the burdens I created for you. You all can write me by sending a letter to Caroline Langley, Fort Laramie, Wyoming Territory. Please wait until you have to make a trip somewhere so that you can mail it from another town. I anxiously await to hear from you. I want you to know that I am happier than I have been in a long time. I miss all of you terribly, but I love the west. The mountains are majestic. You all would love them. Caroline is the daughter and we did not take to each other when I first arrived. In fact, I only took the job to spite her. Somewhere along the way, spite turned to love. I feel as if God has given me a second chance. Caroline is a little spitfire of a thing and keeps me on my toes, but we are very happy together and I hold my own with her. A train runs all the way to Cheyenne and I hope someday you can come and see us. Love, Caleb"

Nils and Olivia were both wiping their eyes by the time Olivia finished reading the letter.

"I feel like the weight of the world is off my shoulders. I've worried so much about that boy. Not only is he alive, but he's happy again," Nils said.

"We really have cause to celebrate now. I can't wait to tell Britt, but we need to be careful and not say anything in front of the children," Olivia warned.

"I can't believe Caleb wrote us that he is in love. He must really be serious about that girl. I didn't think that would ever happen again," Nils said.

"Caleb just needed time for his heart to heal and to meet the right person. I want to meet this Caroline. We need to write Caleb a letter and make a trip to Newbern to mail it. And you need to get to selling horses so that we can go out west in the fall after you get the crops out," Olivia said.

∞

Britt was in the process of rounding up her two children to take them to her parents for the birthday celebration when there came a knock on the door. She opened it to find Albert Roberts standing on the veranda.

Being alone around Albert scared Britt. Truth be told, he even scared her a little when Charles was still alive. Necessity had forced her to see him more than she liked after her daddy talked her into cash renting the farm to the Roberts family in an attempt at a peace offering. The gesture had eased some of the tensions between the families, but still, Britt wasn't going to forget that they sued her for her home, nor would the Roberts forget that Caleb killed Charles.

"Albert, what brings you here?" Britt asked.

"It was time to make a payment on the land rental, and seeing how it's Tyler's birthday, Hazel wanted me to give each of the children a five dollar gold piece," Albert said as he fished the money from his pocket.

"Tyler and Sissy, come here. Grandpa Roberts has something for you," Britt called out, happy to have the children by her side.

Albert handed each child a coin. Tyler looked at the coin in awe and thanked his grandfather. Sissy, still too young to comprehend money, grinned at the shiny object in her hand.

As Albert handed Britt the money for the rent, he asked, "May I have a moment more of your time?"

"What's on your mind?" Britt asked. She tried to look calm, but her heart started racing for what Albert might have to say.

"Hazel is missing the children something fierce since all this has happened. She'd like to come get them Saturday to spend the day with us if you are willing. For that matter, I want to spend some time with them too. They didn't stop being our grandchildren just because Charles died. I promised her that I would ask you," he said.

The request blindsided Britt. Even Hazel had stopped visiting the children after the court case. Britt had assumed that the family would have no further interactions with the children, but Hazel had always treated her well and she knew the children would be looked after proper by their grandmother. "I think that's a good idea. They are Roberts after all," she said.

"Thank you," Albert said. He started to leave and then stopped and turned back towards Britt. "I know that Charles was a sorry husband and that most of it is my fault. He was the baby of the family and I let him get by with way too much. I regret that every day of my life now that he's gone. I don't know what happened between Caleb and Charles. Caleb may have acted in self-defense, but he should have stayed around to clear his name if it were so. I still hold out hope that he's brought to justice someday, but I would like to move on from the bad feelings between us. I shouldn't have tried to break the will."

"Would you have given Caleb a chance to clear his name?" Britt boldly asked.

Albert studied the question a moment. "That's a fair point," he said without actually answering the question.

"I agree that it's time to move on from what has happened," Britt said.

Tipping his hat, Albert left without saying anything more.

Britt grabbed the baked beans she had cooked and herded the children to the wagon. She lifted them up onto the seat and made the drive to her parents' house. As soon as she walked into the kitchen, she could see by her mother's expressions that something had her in a dither. The sight gave Britt a moment of angst as she feared the family had suffered another calamity.

"Come with me," Olivia said as she shepherded Britt to the bedroom while Nils stepped in to entertain his grandchildren.

"Momma, what is it? You're scaring me," Britt said.

Olivia shoved the piece of paper at Britt. We got a letter from Caleb today," she said.

Britt read the letter in a rush and then calmed herself enough to read it again slowly. Her eyes brimmed with tears and she rubbed her hand over her lips before handing the letter back to her mother. "I'm so relieved. I've worried every day that he might be out there dead somewhere and we'd never know what happened to him. And I can tell he's smitten by this Caroline. Caleb's not one to talk about such things on a whim. I'm so happy," she said.

"I know it. I'll sleep like a baby tonight. I pray the bad days are over," Olivia said.

"Me too, Momma," Britt said.

"We better get the party started," Olivia said as she headed towards the kitchen.

Chapter 26

The chill in the morning air hinted that fall's arrival was just around the corner. Caleb and Joey pulled on jackets before riding out to check on the spring foals. They traveled off the ranch into the open range in their search for the mustang herds. On the top of a ridge, they pulled their horses to a stop. Down below stood a stallion with twelve mares, each with a foal.

"Where the wild horses roam," Caleb said with a grin. "This has to be some of the prettiest country in the world. Just cast your eyes on that mountain range to the north. I never get tired of looking at them."

"Looks like the foals made it through the summer just fine. They should be in good shape for the months ahead. Wait until winter does come. Your southern butt is going to gain a whole new appreciation for the word cold," Joey said.

"That's some fine looking stock. I guess out here only the strong ones survive and pass it down the bloodlines," Caleb said, ignoring Joey's southern crack.

"I think you have a point there. I am anxious to see what that stallion of yours sires," Joey said.

"Me too. He's always put his stamp on his prodigy," Caleb noted.

Neither man spoke as they watched the foals frolic about on the grass for a few minutes.

"I'm thinking about asking Claire to marry me," Joey said as casually as if he were picking out a new shirt.

Caleb turned his head, looking at Joey in surprise. "You are? Well, congratulations," he said.

"Claire made it pretty clear from the get-go that she wouldn't wait forever for me," Joey said.

"I guess it's good you know where she stands. No surprises that way," Caleb said.

"You should ask Caroline too. We could have a double wedding," Joey said.

"I haven't known Caroline all that long. You've known Claire forever," Caleb said.

"You've known her long enough to know all you need to know about her. And besides, before long it's going to be too cold to go on your *picnics,*" Joey said.

"What's that supposed to mean?" Caleb asked defensively.

"You know darn well what it means. Claire and I weren't born yesterday. We figured you two out a long time ago. You better make an honest woman out of her before you have no choice in the matter," Joey said.

"I'm glad you're so free with your opinions. I might have to ask for them otherwise," Caleb said.

"I'm just looking out for you and you know it. Let's go find some more foals," Joey said as he nudged his horse into a walk down the ridge.

By the time that the two men made it back to the ranch, Caroline had returned from her trip to town. She sat on the porch waiting for their return wearing her usual men's attire with her hat pulled down so low that seeing her eyes proved nearly impossible.

As Caroline waved an envelope in the air, she said, "I received a letter from Tennessee. I'm guessing it's for you."

Caleb tied his horse in front of the house and hustled up on the porch. He snatched the letter from Caroline and ripped it open. Caroline watched his expression as he read the letter to try to guess the letter's content, but Caleb kept a poker face the whole time.

With the suspense killing her, Caroline said, "Well?"

"Everybody is doing well. Things have gotten better with the Roberts family. Daddy and Momma are going to visit Aunt Ingrid and then take the train out here. They're coming all the way out here," Caleb repeated as if to convince himself.

"That's wonderful. I'll get to meet your parents. I guess I'll have to wear dresses for a while," Caroline said.

As Caleb looked over at Joey standing in the yard, he saw the ranch foreman giving him a stare. Joey's expression all but said, "You better marry her while your folks are here." Caleb gave Joey a wink just to irritate the old rascal.

"How about us going for a ride," Caleb said to Caroline.

"Sure, if you want," Caroline said.

Caleb saddled Buddy for her and the two headed out following the stream. They came to the picnic spot where they had first made love. Caleb stopped his horse and dismounted. Caroline did the same. They walked over to the stream and began skipping rocks across the water.

"It's been quite a year, hasn't it?" Caleb said.

"That it has and none of it I would have guessed in a million years," Caroline said as she slung a rock and watched it skip five times before sinking.

"I started the year in Tennessee never dreaming of coming out west, but here I am, and I've already lived through a range war," he said.

"And look where we started out and where we are now. I really didn't like you," Caroline said with a chuckle.

"No, we didn't hit it off, but I at least noticed that you were pretty," Caleb said and gave her a wink.

"Oh, I noticed you all right. In fact, I think that's part of the reason I didn't like you. I knew you would be a temptation," she said.

The conversation dried up. Caleb desperately tried to think of something to say as he tried to work up his courage. The two of them skipped rocks with the seriousness of a high-stakes poker game.

"Did the ranch do okay selling your horses?" Caleb asked to end the silence.

"We did. Of course, we're carrying two extra men on the payroll now. But I can't very well get rid of Reese and Lucky when they stuck with us through the bad times," she said.

"No, and they're pretty good with horses as long as you let them know what you want. They have also gotten better at training as the summer went on," Caleb said.

"I think they learned a thing or two by watching you. You're pretty good with horses yourself," Caroline teased.

Caleb took a big breath and exhaled. He stepped towards Caroline, pulling her hat from her head. With a toss of it onto the ground, he began pulling the pins from her hair. When he had them all out, he ran his fingers through her mane and shook it out until it fell onto her shoulders. Caroline looked up at him, clearly unsure what he would next do. He took her face into his hands and studied her a moment. Sometimes he still had a hard time believing that he'd found love again and wanted to remember this moment forever.

Dropping down onto one knee, Caleb took her hands into his own. "Caroline, would you marry me? I would love for us to wed while my parents are out here," he said.

Caroline's mouth dropped open and her eyes got big. She pulled her right hand away and covered her mouth for a moment. Reaching down, she stroked Caleb's cheek. "Yes. Yes, Caleb I will marry you."

About the Author

Duane Boehm is a musician, songwriter, and author. He lives on a mini-farm with his wife and an assortment of dogs. Having written short stories throughout his lifetime, he shared them with friends and with their encouragement began his journey as a novelist. Please feel free to email him at boehmduane@gmail.com or like his Facebook Page www.facebook.com/DuaneBoehmAuthor.

Made in the USA
Lexington, KY
13 June 2017